AFTER YOU'VE GONE

AFTER YOU'VE GONE

STORIES BY

ALICE ADAMS

ALFRED A. KNOPF

NEW YORK

1989

THIS IS A BORZOI BOOK
PUBLISHED BY ALFRED A. KNOPF, INC.

Most of the stories in this collection were originally published in the following:
The Boston Globe Magazine, Boulevard, Crosscurrents, New Woman, The New Yorker, The Paris Review, and *Self.* "Favors" was originally published in *Grand Street;* "Lost Cat" in *Image,* and later syndicated by Fiction Network; and "1940: Fall" in *Shenandoah.*

Library of Congress Cataloging-in-Publication Data
Adams, Alice, [date]
After you've gone : stories / by Alice Adams. — 1st ed.
p.   cm.
ISBN 0-394-57926-7
I. Title.
PS3551.D324A69   1989
813'.54—dc20   89-45283   CIP

Manufactured in the United States of America
First Edition

To Til and Charlie Stewart

with much love

CONTENTS

AFTER YOU'VE GONE

AFTER YOU'VE GONE

The truth is, for a while I managed very well indeed. I coped with the house and its curious breakages, and with the bad nights of remembering you only at your best, and the good days suddenly jolted by your ghost. I dealt with the defection of certain old friends, and the crowding-around of a few would-be new best friends. I did very well with all that, in the three months since your departure for Oregon, very well indeed until I began to get these letters from your new person (I reject "lover" as too explicit, and, knowing you, I am not at all sure that "friend" would be applicable). Anyway, Sally Ann.

(You do remember encouraging me to write to you, as somewhat precipitately you announced your departure—as though extending me a kindness? It will make you feel better, you just managed not to say. In any case, with my orderly lawyer's mind, I am putting events—or "matters," as we say—in order.)

The house. I know that it was and is not yours, despite that reckless moment at the Trident (too many margaritas, too

palely glimmering a view of our city, San Francisco) when I
offered to put it in both our names, as joint tenants, which I
literally saw us as, even though it was I who made payments.
However, your two-year occupancy and your incredibly skill-
ful house-husbanding made it seem quite truly yours. (Is this
question metaphysical, rather than legal? If the poet-husband
of a house is not in fact a husband, whose is the house?) But
what I am getting at is this. How could you have arranged for
everything to break the week you left? Even the Cuisinart; no
one else even heard of a broken Cuisinart, ever. And the vac-
uum. And the electric blanket. The dishwasher and the Dis-
posal. Not to mention my Datsun. "Old wiring, these older
flats," the repair person diagnosed my household problems,
adding, "But you've got a beautiful place here," and he ges-
tured across the park—green, pyramidal Alta Plaza, where
even now I can see you running, running, in your eccentric
non-regular-runner outfit: yellow shorts, and that parrot-green
sweatshirt from God knows where, both a little tight.

My Datsun turned out simply to need a tune-up, and since
you don't drive I can hardly blame that on you. Still, the syn-
chronism, everything going at once, was hard not to consider.

Friends. Large parties, but not small dinners, my post-you
invitations ran. Or very small dinners—most welcome, from
single women friends or gay men; unwelcome from wives-away
husbands, or even from probably perfectly nice single men. I
am just not quite up to all that yet.

People whom I had suspected of inviting us because of your
poet fame predictably dropped off.

Nights. In my dreams of course you still are here, or you are
leaving and I know that you are, and there is nothing to do to
stop you (you have already told me, so sadly, about Sally Ann,
and the houseboat in Portland). Recently I have remembered
that after my father died I had similar dreams; in those dreams

he was dying, I knew, yet I could not keep him alive. But those father dreams have a guilty sound, I think, and I truly see no cause for guilt on my part toward you. I truly loved you, in my way, and I did what I could (I thought) to keep us happy, and I never, never thought we would last very long. Isn't two years a record of sorts for you, for maybe any non-marrying poet? Sometimes I thought it was simply San Francisco that held you here, your City Lights–Tosca circuit, where you sought out ghosts of Beats. Well, in my dreams you are out there still, or else you are here with me in our (my) bed, and we awaken slowly, sleepily to love.

Once, a month or so ago, I thought I saw you sitting far back in a courtroom; I saw those damn black Irish curls and slanted eyes, your big nose and arrogant chin, with that cleft. A bad shock, that; for days I wondered if it actually could have been you, your notion of a joke, or some sort of test.

In all fairness, though—and since I mention it I would like to ask you something. Just why did my efforts at justice, even at seeing your side of arguments, so enrage you? I can hear you shouting: "Why do you have to be so goddam *fair,* what *is* this justice of yours?"

But as I began to say, in all fairness I have to concede that I miss your cooking. On the nights that you cooked, that is. I really liked your tripe soup and your special fettuccine with all those wild mushrooms. And the Sunday scrambled eggs that we never got to till early afternoon.

And you are a marvel at fixing things, even if they have a tendency not to stay fixed.

And, most importantly, a first-rate poet; Yale and now the Guggenheim people seem to think so, and surely as you hope the MacArthur group will come around. Having read so little poetry other than yours, I am probably no judge; however, as I repeatedly told you, to me it was magic, pure word-alchemy.

I do miss it all, the house-fixing and cooking, the love and poetry. But I did very well without it all. Until recently.

The letters. The first note, on that awful forget-me-not paper, in that small, tight, rounded hand, was a prim little apology: she felt badly about taking you away from me (a phrase from some junior high school, surely) but she also felt sure that I would "understand," since I am such a fair-minded person (I saw right off that you had described my habits of thought in some detail). I would see that she, a relatively innocent person, would have found your handsomeness-brilliance-sexiness quite irresistible (at that point I wondered if you could have written the letter yourself, which still seems a possibility). She added that naturally by now I would have found a replacement for you, the natural thing for a woman like me, in a city like San Francisco. That last implication, as to the loose life-styles both of myself and of San Francisco, would seem to excuse the two of you fleeing to the innocence of Portland, Oregon.

A couple of false assumptions lay therein, however. Actually, in point of fact, I personally might do better, man-wise, in Portland than down here. The men I most frequently meet are young lawyers, hard-core yuppies, a group I find quite intolerable, totally unacceptable, along with the interchangeable young brokers—real-estate dealers and just plain dealers. Well, no wonder that I too took up with a poet, an out-of-shape man with no CDs or portfolio but a trunk full of wonderful books. (I miss your books, having got through barely half of them. And did you really have to take the *Moby-Dick* that I was in the middle of? Well, no matter; I went out to the Green Apple and stocked up, a huge carton of books, the day you left.)

In any case, I felt that she, your young person, your Sally Ann, from too much evidence had arrived at false conclusions.

In some ways we are more alike, she and I, than she sees. I too was a setup, a perfect patsy for your charm, your "difference."

But why should she have been told so much about me at all? Surely you must have a few other topics; reading poems aloud as you used to do with me would have done her more good, or at least less harm, I believe. But as I pondered this question, I also remembered several of our own conversations, yours and mine, having to do with former lovers. It was talk that I quite deliberately cut short, for two clear reasons: one, I felt an odd embarrassment at my relative lack of what used to be called experience; and, two, I did not want to hear about yours. You did keep on trying, though; there was one particular woman in New York, a successful young editor (though on a rather junky magazine, as I remember), a woman you wanted me to hear all about, but I would not. "She has nothing to do with us," I told you (remember?). It now seems unfortunate that your new young woman, your Sally Ann, did not say the same about me.

Next came a letter which contained a seemingly innocent question: should Sally Ann go to law school, what did I think? On the surface this was a simple request for semi-expert advice; as she went on and on about it, though, and on and on, I saw that she was really asking me how she could turn herself into me, which struck me as both sad and somewhat deranged. Assuming that you have an ideal woman on whom Sally Ann could model herself, I am hardly that woman. You don't even much like "lady lawyers," as in some of your worst moments you used to phrase it.

Not having answered the first note at all (impossible; what could I have said?), I responded to this one, because it seemed required, with a typed postcard of fairly trite advice: the hard work involved, the overcrowding of the field, the plethora of even token women.

. . .

And now she had taken to writing me almost every day; I
mean it, at least every other day. Does she have no other
friends? No relatives, even, or old school ties? If she does, in
her present state of disturbance they have faded from her mind
(poor, poor Sally Ann, all alone with you, in Portland, on a
Willamette River houseboat), and only I remain, a purely
accidental, non-presence in her life.

The rains have begun in Portland, and she understands that
they will continue throughout the winter. She does not really
like living on a houseboat, she finds it frightening; the boat
rocks, and you have told her that all boats rock, there is nothing to be done. (You must be not exactly in top form either.
I never heard you admit to an inability to remedy anything
—even my Datsun; you said you could fix it and you did,
temporarily.)

You have found some old friends over at Reed College, she
tells me; you hang out a lot over there, and you tell her that
she would be very much happier with a job. Very likely she
would, but you have taken her to an extremely high unemployment area.

She doesn't understand your poetry at all, and doesn't know
what to say when you read it to her. Well, this is certainly a
problem that I too could have had, except that I dealt with it
head-on, as it were, simply and clearly saying that I didn't
understand poetry, that I had not read much or ever studied
it. But that to me your poems sounded marvelous—which
they did; I really miss the sound of them, your words.

You talk about me more and more.

You are at home less and less. And now Sally Ann confesses
to me that she used to be a waitress at the Tosca; on some of
the nights when I was at home, here in San Francisco (actually

I used to be grateful for a little time to catch up on work),
when I assumed you were just hanging out in North Beach,
you were actually courting Sally Ann, so to speak. Well, at
this point I find this new information quite painless to absorb;
it simply makes me miss you even less. But Sally Ann wonders
if I think you could possibly be seeing someone else now? She
says that you've mentioned a French professor at Reed, a most
talented woman, you've said. Do I think—?

Well, I most certainly do think; you seem to prefer women
with very respectable professions, poor Sally Ann representing
the single rule-proving exception, I suppose. Some sort of
lapse in calculation on your part—or quite likely Sally Ann
had more to do with me than with herself, if you see what I
mean, and I think you will. In any case, a fatal error all
around.

Because it is clear to me that in an emotional sense you are
battering this young woman. She is being abused by you. I
could prove it to a jury. And, unlike me, she is quite without
defenses.

You must simply knock it off. For one thing, it's beneath
you, as you surely in your better, saner, kinder moments must
clearly see (you're not all bad; even in my own worst moments
I recall much good, much kindness, even). Why don't you just
give her a ticket to somewhere, along with some gentle, ego-
preserving words (heaven knows you're at your best with
words), and let her go? Then you can move in your Reed College French professor and live happily there on your houseboat—almost forever, at least until the Portland rains let up
and you feel like moving on.

As for myself, it seems only fair to tell you that I have
indeed found a new friend—or, rather, an old friend has re-
appeared in my life in another role. (*Fair.* As I write this, I
wonder if in some way, maybe, you were right all along to

object to my notion of fairness? There was always a slightly hostile getting-even element in my justice? Well, I will at least admit that possibility.) In any case, I am taking off on a small trip to Jackson, Wyoming, day after tomorrow, with my old-new friend. About whom I can only at this moment say so far so good, in fact very good indeed—although I have to admit that I am still a little wary, after you. However, at least for me he is a more known quality than you were (we were undergraduates together, in those distant romantic Berkeley days), and I very much doubt that you'll be getting any letter of complaint regarding me. He already knows what he's getting, so to speak.

And so, please wish me well, as I do you (I'll keep my fingers crossed for the MacArthur thing).

And, I repeat, let Sally Ann go. All three of us, you, me, and Sally Ann, will be much better off—you without her, and she without you. And me without the crazy burden of these letters, which, if I were *really* fair, I would send on to you.

1940: FALL

"Hasn't anyone noticed those clouds? They're incredibly beautiful." These words were spoken with some despair, for indeed no one had noticed, by a woman named Caroline Gerhardt, on a late evening in September, 1940. Caroline Coffin Gerhardt, actually, or so she signed the many letters that she wrote to newspapers, both local and further afield: the *Capitol Times,* right there in Madison, Wisconsin, and Colonel McCormick's infamous (Caroline's word) Chicago *Tribune.*

The ponderously shifting, immense white clouds contemplated by Caroline were moving across an enormous black sky, above one of Madison's smaller lakes. This house, Caroline's, was perched up on a fairly high bluff, yielding views of the dark water in which the reflected clouds were exaggerated, distorted by the tiny flicker of the waves. There was also a large full moon, but full moons—at least to Caroline— seemed much less remarkable than those clouds.

No one else in the room noticed anything remarkable, because almost all of them, all much younger than Caroline, were dancing slowly, slowly, body to body, to some slow, very sexy recorded music. The "children," as Caroline thought of these steamy adolescents, especially her own two girls, have only taken romantic notice of the moon. Beautiful raven-haired Amy Gerhardt, who resembles her absent father rather than smaller, pale, and somewhat wispy Caroline—Amy's perfectly painted lips have just grazed her partner's ear as she whispered, "You see? Another full moon. That makes seven since February." The boy pressed her more tightly into his own body. All those tall boys and smooth-haired, gardenia-smelling girls danced too closely, Caroline had observed, with pain. Hardly dancing at all. Six or eight couples, two or three stags, in the big, low-ceilinged, pine-paneled room—the game room. Dancing, their eyes half closed, not looking out to the lake, to the moon and sky.

Caroline's letters to the papers had to do with the coming war, with what Caroline saw as its clear necessity: Hitler must be stopped. The urgency of it possessed her, what Hitler was doing to the Jews, the horror of it always in her mind. And the smaller countries, systematically devastated. There in the isolationist Midwest she was excoriated as a warmonger (small, gentle, peaceable Caroline). Or worse: more than once—dirty toilet paper in the mail.

She also received from quite other sources pictures that were just beginning to be smuggled out of the camps. Buchenwald, Dachau.

She was actively involved in trying to help the refugees who had begun to arrive in Madison, with housing, jobs, sometimes at the university.

There was in fact a refugee boy at the party in Caroline's game room that night. Egon Heller, the son of an anti-Nazi editor, now dead in Auschwitz. Egon and his mother had arrived from England. Hearing of them, going over to see them, and liking the mother (able actually to help her with a translator job), Caroline impulsively invited the boy. "If you're not busy tonight, there's a little party at my house. My daughters—about your age. They're both at Wisconsin High. Oh, you too? Oh, good."

Egon seemed more English than German. "The years of formation," his mother explained. Tall and shy, long-nosed and prominent of tooth, he seemed much younger than he was— younger, that is, than American boys his age. Not adolescent, more childlike. One of the three young people not dancing just then, Egon stood near the record player, in the proximity of Caroline's younger daughter, Julie—plump and brilliant and not yet discovered by boys (Caroline's idea being that she surely would be, and soon)—although Julie was extremely "well liked," as the phrase then went, in high school. By boys and girls, and teachers.

Caroline's secret conviction about her daughter was that within Julie's flesh were embedded her own genes, her sensuality. The intense dark impulses that had enmeshed her with Arne Gerhardt and landed her with three children—the youngest, now upstairs asleep, born embarrassingly only a year ago, when Caroline was already over forty.

Caroline felt with Julie a sensual kinship and consequent cause for alarm far more than with more overtly sexy Amy, the oldest. Caroline too had once been plump and brilliant and shy.

Maybe this Egon will be the one, romantic Caroline thought, looking toward the corner to Egon and Julie, who so far seemed to have in common only the fact of not dancing. He's so tall and thin and toothy, Julie now so unsmiling, so matter-of-fact. Still, it would be very nice, thought Caroline. English–Jewish–New England–Swedish grandchildren—she would like that very much.

The other young person not dancing in the early part of that evening was a new girl in town, from Julie's class, invited by Julie (who would later be strongly maternal, Caroline knew). A strange-looking girl from Oklahoma, with an odd accent and a funny name: Lauren. Most striking of all about Lauren, right off, was her hair—very pale, more white than blond, it stood out all over her head in tiny fine soft ringlets.

She looked younger than the rest of the girls, perhaps partly because she did not wear lipstick. Her mouth was long and finely drawn, and pale, in that roomful of girls. Even Julie had dark blood-red lips. A very tall, very thin girl, her neck was long and she moved her head about uncertainly, watching the dancers. Her smile was slightly crooked, off.

Someone should ask her to dance, thought Caroline. How rude these children are, how entirely selfish. Perhaps Egon will, that would be very nice, two strangers finding each other. But maybe he is too polite to ask Lauren with Julie standing there; he doesn't know that Julie wouldn't mind in the least being left alone. She will probably be going up soon to see about Baby.

Seeing no way out of this social dilemma, but fated always to feel responsible, Caroline herself began to move in Lauren's direction—not easy, as the music had become more lively, people hopping about and arms and legs thrust out. Slowly making her way, Caroline tried to think of social-welcoming-maternal conversation.

"So you and Julie are taking Latin together?" Reaching Lauren at last, this breathless, silly remark was all she had been able to summon up finally.

"Yes. Cicero. There's only five of us in the class." Lauren laughed apologetically, as though abashed at the small size of the Latin class. But then, her huge eyes on Caroline, she said earnestly, "This is the most beautiful room I've ever seen. The view—"

Unprepared for intensity, Caroline was flustered. "Well, it's a funny old house. Not exactly practical. But it is nice, being here on the lake."

"I love it in Madison." Lauren's voice was rapt, those huge pale eyes burned. Caroline sensed that the girl had not said this before, to anyone. It was not a remark to be made to contemporaries, other children.

"Well, yes, it is a very nice town," Caroline agreed. "Especially the lakes, and the university." Some flicker of intelligent response across Lauren's face made her add, "A very conservative place, though, on the whole."

"Try Enid, Oklahoma," Lauren laughed quickly. "More backward than conservative. But I know what you mean. The whole Midwest. Especially now."

Was the girl simply parroting remarks overheard at home, or were those ideas of her own? Impossible to tell, but in any case Caroline found herself liking this Lauren, wanting to talk to her.

However, just at the moment of Caroline wanting to speak, forming sentences in her mind, the two of them were interrupted by a tall, fair, thin boy—Caroline knew him, knew his parents, but could not for the moment recall his name. Thick light hair, distinctively heavy eyebrows above deepset dark blue eyes. To Lauren he said, "Care to dance this one?" And then, somewhat perfunctorily (still, he did say it), "Okay with you, Mrs. Gerhardt?" He was staring at Lauren.

And they were gone, off and out into the room, lost among other couples, Lauren and Tommy Russell (his name had just come to Caroline, of course). And before she could collect herself or even could turn to watch them, from far upstairs she heard Baby's urgent cry. Bottle time. Glancing toward Julie, observing that she and Egon had at last begun to talk, Caroline signaled to her daughter that she would go up. "I want to get to bed early anyway," Caroline mouthed above the music, smiling, as she headed for the kitchen. For milk, a clean bottle, a heating saucepan.

Good Baby, the easiest child of the three, subsided as soon as she heard her mother's footsteps on the stairs. Smiling up from her crib, she grasped the proffered bottle, clamped it into her mouth as Caroline settled into the adjacent battered easy chair.

From here, upstairs, she had an even better view of the lake, and the moon and the marvelous white clouds, and Caroline then felt an unaccustomed peace possess her. She thought, It *is* easier with Arne away (a fact hitherto not quite acknowledged). Generally his absences were only troubling: *would* he come back? That year he had a visiting professorship at Stanford, two years before at Virginia.

Now, as she peacefully crooned to the milk-smelling, half-asleep fair child, she thought that this time even if Arne decided to take off for good, she would really be all right, she and her three girls, who themselves were more than all right—they were going to be great women, all three. She could cope with the house, the good big lakefront place bought so cheaply ten years back. They would all be perfectly okay, Amy with her heady romances and her disappointing grades, Julie with her perfect grades, and perhaps a new beau in this nice English-German boy, this Egon. And maybe a nice new friend in this Lauren Whitfield, from Enid, Oklahoma. And Baby will always be fine, thought Caroline, sleepily.

And Roosevelt will win the election and declare war on Germany within the year, and we will win that war in a matter of months. Hitler defeated. Dead. Maybe tortured in a concentration camp.

Caroline thought all that, still crooning to Baby, and smiling secretly, somnolently to herself.

. . .

Lauren Whitfield, the new girl with the funny hair, and Julie Gerhardt did indeed become friends, though not quite of the sort that Caroline had envisioned. They began going to lunch at the Rennebohm's drugstore across from the school, and Julie, sensing Lauren's extreme interest in what was to her a glamorous new place, became a sort of balladeer, a chronicler of high-school love affairs, past and present. Disastrous break-ups, the occasional betrayal. Along with a detailed rundown on the current situation, who was going with whom as this new season began, this warm and golden fall.

Over thick chocolate malteds and English muffins, Julie told Lauren everything she wanted to know, or nearly, including the story of Julie's own sister, Amy the beautiful, with whom boys quite regularly fell in love. "She was just having a good time, her sophomore year, really getting around. But the phone calls! Arne threatened to have the phone cut off, he has a pretty short temper. And then during spring vacation she met Nelson Manning, he was home from Dartmouth, much too old for her, about nineteen. But they fell madly in love, flowers all the time, and after he went back to school those letters. And more flowers, and phone calls! Poor Amy spent that whole spring fighting with Caroline and Arne. But she sort of won, I think mostly just wearing them down. So that when Nelson came home in June she got to see him. Under certain conditions. Well, she sneaked out and saw him a lot more than they ever knew about. Nelson was entirely insane over Amy, he wanted to quit school and get married right away. But of course Amy wasn't about to do that, and so in the fall he went back to Dartmouth and she moped around and then suddenly no more letters. No flowers. Another girl back there, probably someone at Vassar or one of those places, we're sure it must have been. Caro and I were truly worried about her. Moping all day, not eating. But gradually she began to go out a little, and then over Christmas she got sort of serious about Jeff, and they started going steady in February. Full-moon time. But there are still certain songs she can't hear without crying. 'All the Things You Are' is one. She's not *really* over Nelson."

Nothing like that had ever gone on in Enid, not that Lauren had ever heard about.

And then, "I think Tommy Russell is really interested in you," Julie told Lauren.

So much for the intellectual friendship that Caroline Gerhardt had envisioned between her brilliant middle daughter and Lauren Whitfield, the bright new girl in town. But even had she been aware of the content of those endless conversations Caroline would really not have cared, so entirely absorbed was she in her own despair: her desperation over what was going on, still, in Germany.

Even the Midwestern press had by now conceded that Roosevelt would win the election, and would get the country into that European war—wasteful, unnecessary. But Caroline often felt that it would be too late, too late for murdered Jews, for devastated Poland. Holland. Fallen France.

She continued her impassioned but well-reasoned letters to the press, along with occasional gay (she hoped for gaiety) small notes to Arne, in response to his occasional cards from California.

Caroline Coffin, from Vermont, and Arne Gerhardt, from northern Wisconsin, Door County, met at Oberlin College in the early twenties, and both at that time were filled with, inspired by, the large-spirited ideals of that institution. Big, dark, clumsy (but very brilliant, Caroline thought) Arne, enthusiastic about the new League of Nations, and smaller, fairer Caroline, who was then, as now, dedicated to peace, the abolition of war. Young and passionately in love, together they read Emma Goldman, Bertrand Russell—and moved into an apartment together. Caroline became pregnant, and a week before the birth of Amy they yielded to their parents and got married.

"Lauren Whitfield is going steady with Tommy Russell," Julie reported to her mother at breakfast on Saturday morning. They were both feeding Baby, alternating spoonfuls of cereal with scrambled eggs, which was Baby's preferred method. Amy slept upstairs, on into the day.

"Isn't that rather sudden?" Caroline was a little surprised at the censoriousness with which she herself spoke.

"Oh yes, everyone thinks it's terribly romantic. He asked her on their first date."

Impossible for Caroline to gauge the content of irony in her daughter's voice. "I somehow thought she was more—" Caroline then could not finish her own sentence, and she realized that she had to a considerable degree already lost interest in this conversation, a thing that seemed to happen to her far too often.

"You thought she was more intelligent?" Knowing her mother well, Julie supplied the missing bias. "Actually she's extremely smart, but she's sort of, uh, dizzy. Young. Her parents are breaking up, that's why she's here with her grandparents. They drink a lot, her parents."

"Poor girl."

"Yes. Well, anyway, she's bright but she's not all intellectual. Yet."

. . .

Julie herself did not go out a lot with boys that year. But she seemed both busy and contented. She studied hard and read a lot, at home she helped Caroline with Baby. She also functioned as a sort of occasional secretary for her mother, opening mail and often shielding Caroline from extreme isolationist vituperation.

And Julie and Egon Heller, the German-English refugee boy, did become friends, of sorts, if not in the romantic way that Caroline had hoped. Their friendship was in fact remarked upon, so unusual was it in those days of rigidly coded adolescent behavior. Simply, they spent a lot of time together, Egon and Julie. They could be seen whispering over their books in study hall, though very possibly about assignments. Never holding hands, no touching, nothing like that. Sometimes they went to the movies together, but usually on a Saturday afternoon, sometimes with Baby along. Not at night, not a date.

Very odd, was what most people observing them thought. But then exceptionally bright children were often odd; psychologists said so.

Caroline heard from Arne in a somewhat longer than usual postcard that he would not, after all, be coming home to Madison for Christmas, for a number of reasons; money, time, and work were cited. Nothing very original by way of an excuse.

But Caroline, who had painful premonitions of just this announcement, reacted with a large sense of relief. To her own great surprise. Oh, *good,* is what she thought. I won't have to make a lot of Christmas fuss—or not Arne's kind of fuss. No big parties, and I won't have to try to look wonderful all the time. And worry that he's drinking too much and making passes at undergraduate girls. I can just do the things I like, that he thinks are dumb. I can bake cookies, maybe run up a new formal for Amy. (Caroline had a curious dramatic flair for making certain clothes. Highly successful with evening things, she had never done well with the small flannel nightgowns, for example, that other women did in no time.) I can read a lot, she thought. And I'll go for a lot of walks in the snow.

The snows had come somewhat earlier than usual to Madison that year. Soon after the first of November (just after the election), serious snowfalls began, blanketing the steeply sloped university campus, causing traffic trouble in the streets—and making life far more wonderful for all children, including those in high school.

Couples on dates went tobogganing on the vast golf course of the Black Hawk Country Club, an endless hill, just dangerous enough to provide a long intensely satisfying thrill. And couples who had parked on other hills to neck, in the marvelous privacy of deep snowbanks, could emerge to observe a curious pink light on all the surrounding miles of white, reflected in all the lakes.

Lauren Whitfield and Tommy Russell spent considerable time in his car, in that way. They marveled both at each other (so much in love) and at the loveliness of snow, which Lauren had never really seen before.

.   .   .

Caroline's kitchen was hung with rows of copper pots, enthusiastically bought in Paris, in the flea market, on Arne and Caroline's honeymoon (with baby Amy in tow). Never polished, they were now all dark and dull, black-grimed. The blue Mexican tile around the sink, from an attempted second honeymoon, this time without Amy but on which Julie was conceived—the tile had fared somewhat better; though cracked, it retained a bright brave color.

On the afternoon that Caroline had chosen for Christmas-cookie baking, by the time the children arrived from school there were already smells of burned sugar, and spilled flour on the floor into which Baby continually crawled. Julie had brought both Lauren Whitfield and Egon Heller.

"Egon, and Lauren! How very nice to see you. These days I hardly ever." Floury, flustered Caroline made effusive welcoming gestures, to which Egon responded with one of his curious stiff bows (he actually bowed), and a smile.

Julie took over the problem of keeping Baby out of the general mess, and Caroline divided her attention between the cookies, which she judged still salvageable, and an intense old argument with Egon, about Roosevelt.

"But he's always—"

"But what you fail to grasp—"

"People of his social class—"

Lauren seemed quiet, preoccupied and sad, Caroline observed, with a certain impatience. Adolescents are simply very, very self-absorbed, she thought.

To Egon she said, positively, "Roosevelt will soon declare war on Germany, and he will be able to win it very quickly. And I know a man who's in a position to know things who tells me that the Nazi-Soviet pact can't last, not possibly. The Russians will come in on our side. Our strongest allies."

.   .   .

"Lauren and Tommy Russell have broken up," Julie told her mother one night in February as together they did the supper dishes, Baby being asleep and Amy out.

"Wasn't that rather quick? You just told me, I thought . . ." Caroline heard her own voice trail off into vagueness.

"Quick and strange. She can't quite say what happened, or she won't. She just cries a lot. Like when Amy and Nelson broke up."

"That's too bad," Caroline began to say, and then did not, as she recognized that in truth she had almost no sympathy for the broken hearts of the very young. "That girl seems to be rushing through her life at quite a rate" was her more sincere comment.

"I think she'll be okay eventually. It may just take a while." Judicious Julie.

"When I think of Tito's brave Partisans," wrote Caroline to the *Capitol Times* (Madison), with copies to the Chicago *Tribune,* the Des Moines *Register,* and the Moline *Dispatch.* She thought of the San Francisco *Chronicle* or even the Palo Alto *Times* (where Arne was) but she censored that impulse as frivolous. Also, they would probably not print letters from an unknown woman in Wisconsin. And anyway, California went for Roosevelt.

Actually, Caroline was managing considerable detachment from Arne these days, this early and acutely beautiful spring.

Long walks were a reliable cure for her troubled sleep, she found, and so every afternoon for an hour or so she walked around the lake, noting pussywillows at the muddy edges of the water, where small gentle waves lapped, very slowly. And sudden secret wildflowers in what had been a small neglected meadow. And at the bottom of her garden (also neglected) early iris, wild and bright.

She began to sleep better. Or if she should wake up she could read. One of the joys of singleness, she told herself; you don't have to worry about the other person's sleep, along with your own.

June 22, 1941, was the day on which Hitler's troops attacked Soviet Russia. No more Nazi-Soviet pact. The Russians were now our valiant allies. (It was also Lauren Whitfield's last day in Madison. Back to Enid, Oklahoma.)

Possibly more than anyone else in Madison, Caroline Coffin Gerhardt was moved to celebrate this clear beginning of the end of Hitler. She wanted a party, but from the beginning nothing worked out in terms of this festive impulse. No one even remotely appropriate was available. Vacations had begun, varieties of other plans. Even her children failed her: Amy was off dancing with her beau, and Julie was to have an early farewell supper with Lauren and her grandparents.

Caroline's happy day was further marred by news from Arne: a postcard (so typical) announcing his imminent arrival. "I've missed all my girls." Well, I'll bet he has, was Caroline's sour reaction. Who else would put up with such a selfish bastard?

We will have to work out a much more independent life from each other, Caroline thought, over the small steak that she had bought for her solitary celebration (*not* black market: her month's ration), as she sipped from the split of Beaujolais, an even greater treat.

I should not have Arne so continually in my mind, she told

herself. That's what the children do, they think only of themselves and their impassioned sexual lives.

The important fact is that the end of Hitler's evil has now
begun.

Epilogue: San Diego, California. The middle eighties.

The man at the next table at this almost empty semi-
Polynesian restaurant is not even slightly interested in her,
thinks Lauren Whitfield, now a tall, gray-blond, very well
dressed woman, a psychologist, well known for several books.

She is in fact on a tour for her latest book, having to do
with alcoholic co-dependency. She reached San Diego a day
early, hoping for a rest. On her way to her room, across a series
of tropically planted lawns she observed an Olympic pool, and
she thought, Oh, very good. And seated next to the pool,
though fully dressed, she saw this same tall man, whom she
had also seen at the reservation desk. Coming into the dining
room just now, he smiled very politely, if coldly, acknowledging these small accidental encounters.

Lauren is quite used to book tours, by now. Living alone in
New York after the lengthy demise of her second marriage, she
rather likes the adventure of trips, the novelty of unfamiliar
scenery, new faces. She quite often falls into conversation with
other single travelers, such encounters providing at the worst
only a few bored hours. More frequently she has felt warm
stirrings of interest, of possible friendship. On far rarer occa-
sions, sex.

But this tall, too thin, nearsighted, and not well dressed
European intellectual keeps his large nose pushed clearly into
his book. Lauren has observed him with some care, over all of
their small encounters, and is quite sure that they could find

areas of common interest, some shared opinions. Their political views, she would bet, would be similar.

Sex is out; in a sexual way she is not drawn to him in the least. But so often men are slow to perceive that overtures of any sort are not necessarily sexual in nature. Lauren ponders this sad and trouble-causing human fact as she also thinks, Well, hell, I'd really like an hour or so of conversation. Coffee. Damn his book.

And then, as she stares (he is so entirely unaware of her that she is able to stare with impunity), a small flash goes off within the deep recesses of her mind, so that she is able, with great confidence, and a smile that she knows is appealing, slightly crooked and not *too* self-assured, to tap his elbow and to say, "Excuse me, but aren't you Egon Heller?"

Perfectly calm, as though used to being thus accosted (possibly he is somewhat famous too, used to being recognized? or a professor, with old students sometimes showing up? or both?), Egon lowers his book very patiently, and very politely he tells her that yes, that is his name. And then, with the very slightest English-German accent, he asks her, "But have we met?"

"Yes, but terribly long ago. At the Gerhardts'. In Madison, Wisconsin."

Now Egon does look quite startled, and confused, so much so that he drops his book as he stands and extends a smooth cool strong hand to Lauren. "At the Gerhardts'! Extraordinary."

"Yes, in the fall of 1940. You'd just got there, I think, and I had just moved to Madison. But do sit down. Coffee?"

"Yes, thank you." He does sit down, now smiling warmly, attractively.

Lauren asks him, right off, "Do you ever go back to Madison? I always wonder what happened to Julie Gerhardt. My favorite friend."

At this, quite startlingly Egon begins to laugh, in a choking, ratchety way that reddens his face, and it is some minutes before he is able to say, "Well, one of the things that happened to her is that she married me, in 1947. And another thing, or five other, is our children. We have five, the last one thank God just out of graduate school. And another—I know I should have said this first—she has her doctorate in math. From the University of Chicago. Very hard on her, doing all that at once." Egon smiles with such sympathy, such unambivalent admiration that Lauren is more than a little envious (neither of her husbands had much use for her work). As well as touched.

She says, "Well, I love that news, that's wonderful. And it's so amazing that I ran into you. By the way, I'm Lauren Whitfield, I just lived in Madison that one year."

Obviously not remembering her (if he noticed her at all, he must have thought her just another blond, boy-crazy American girl, which Lauren will now concede that she was), Egon politely says, "Oh, of course," and proceeds to tell her more Gerhardt news.

Amy has been married three times but seems at last to have settled down with a man whom Egon describes as a really nice fellow (Lauren has the sense, though, that Egon, so visibly nice himself, has said that about all the husbands). Baby— and now Egon's face lengthens and saddens—Baby died in the early sixties. Drugs.

Lauren: "Oh dear. So in a way Baby was always Baby." She has been unable not to say that.

"Quite." Egon frowns, and then his face brightens as he asks, "You remember Caroline, the mother?"

"Of course, she was wonderful. I always wanted to know her more."

Caroline, still very much alive at eighty-something, is even more wonderful now, Egon tells Lauren. She still writes letters to papers, to congressmen and senators, and she goes to demonstrations, *still:* for disarmament, against military involvement, anywhere. She has been honored by national peace organizations; he names several. "Most of the time she feels quite well," Egon says. "A little trouble with her back, some other small problems, but she is for the most part all right."

Arne died a long time ago, in the fifties.

Digesting all this news, which has mostly made her smile with pleasure, Lauren is quiet for a while, stirring and drinking her coffee very slowly, before she asks him, "Tell me, do you happen to know anything about someone named Tommy Russell?"

"No, I don't think so. But the name, something comes. A football star, in high school?"

"Basketball. He was very thin. Blond."

Egon frowns. "No. Now nothing comes."

Surprised at the depth of her disappointment, and afraid that it will show, Lauren tells him, "I, uh, went steady with him for a while that year. And then one night he got really drunk, and I was really scared, and I couldn't tell anyone. And my parents—"

She sees that she has completely lost his interest. A polite glaze has replaced the animation with which Egon described the new-old Caroline and the accomplishments of Julie. And Lauren senses that actually they do not have a great deal more to say to each other. "Such ancient history!" she comments.

"But you must come to see us," Egon next (somewhat surprisingly) says to her. "Julie would be so pleased, I know, and

Caroline. Did I say that we are all still there in that same house on the bluff? The house you remember?"

"No, you didn't but that's really great. I will come, what a wonderful idea."

And, sitting there among the fake South Sea Island masks and the real but derelict, neglected tropical plants, Lauren tries to reimagine that house in Madison. How the lake looked at night.

THE END OF THE WORLD

Zelda Hoskins, a pretty, light-haired young woman from Toronto, is seated on the balcony of her hotel room, far south, in the Mexican tropics. At the moment, she is contemplating the small quick black butterflies in the shrubbery next to her terrace: an occasional monarch, and a couple of large, very fluttery pure white ones. She watches as a tiny green-black hummingbird zooms from nowhere to the bush of red flowers, ignoring the amber-yellow bougainvillea that Zelda especially admires. She has thought of that particular color in Canada. Would it be there still? During all the heavy-ended, frozen Canadian months that preceded this trip she has imagined the yellow bougainvillea, and butterflies, hummingbirds.

And even now that she is here, those long leaden cold days are very much in Zelda's mind. A Toronto winter. She sees herself there, dreaming of Mexico, of here. Dreams of flowers and warmth and the glittery sea.

Or perhaps this is still the dream? Perhaps actually she is now in Toronto, only dreaming of Mexico? In the unreal warmth she shivers. She finds such speculations interesting, though slightly scaring. And dangerous, really. She knows that she should simply savor being here. She should concentrate on these given moments, even try to slow their passage. After all, they will only be here for a week.

But it is very hard to accept the fact of being where you have dreamed of; Zelda begins to see that. Like the troubles of love, the difficulty of actually being with the longed-for person, when you have spent so many hours imagining how it will be.

Yes, that is exactly what it is like. Like love, an extremity of love. Zelda sighs, and yields to thoughts of her lover, a young man whom Zelda loves extremely. Who is now in Toronto, or maybe he is back in New York, where he lives. In any case, not with her.

Inside their room Abe Hoskins is almost ready to go to breakfast, to which he very much looks forward: the piles of fresh fruit, and the Mexican rolls, *bolillos,* that he especially likes.

Abe in fact relishes the whole episode of breakfast, the walk from their room on the narrow pathway, with the view of the beach and the ocean, sometimes boats. And the other view, to their right, of banks of flowers. And then the look of the dining room itself, the sea seen through heavy waving palms, and the waiting white beach below.

He even enjoys bargaining for newspapers with the small, wiry brown Mexican newsboys, one especially—Gabino, an appealing, very quick-witted kid with an odd, twisted, reluctant smile. Last winter, with considerable trouble, Abe mailed the pair of tennis shoes (high, white) that Gabino had made it clear he very much wanted (with pictures and sign language:

the Hoskinses do not speak Spanish). Abe drew all around Gabino's foot on some writing paper, and took the drawing to the store in Toronto. Bought, packaged, mailed, and he never heard from Gabino. He wonders if Gabino will show up this year, and if he ever got the package.

"It's really clouded over," Zelda and Abe say to each other as together they emerge from their room and begin the walk toward breakfast.

"Look," Zelda says next.

She means the rising, arching plants that now line their pathway. Feathery greenery, against what had been a bare embankment. An archway of green, making a ceremony of their progress that first day.

But above them the sky is hung with clouds, pale, cottony, in a sky that is always simply clear and blue.

"It never rains?" says Zelda.

"It could. But more likely a fantastic sunset," Abe assures her.

Evelyn Fisk, from Washington, D.C., also comes to this hotel for a week each winter, and although her weeks often overlap with those of the Hoskinses, they have so far exchanged only the most tentative looks of recognition. Evelyn, Mrs. Fisk, is a large middle-aged woman, her face broad and pleasant, her short white hair shaped smoothly to her head. She is always alone on these trips, but something about her prohibits the sort of overtures that such "single" people can invite, a look of self-sufficiency, perhaps, or of sheer absorption in private concerns—of which she has in fact a great many: a large and demanding family, and more recently an involvement with the sanctuary movement.

This annual trip to Mexico is actually a sort of present she has awarded to herself for years of service: thirty-odd years of marriage to Grantly Fisk, a Midwestern senator prominent in Washington. A busy liberal: Evelyn supports his views, although very much disliking the public life that his work requires. Grantly refers to these trips as Evelyn's "time off for good behavior," by which she is only half amused. She no longer gives much thought to her actual feelings about her husband. At this point, as she sees it, what could possibly be gained by such a dissection?

In Washington she usually manages to avoid the press, which by this time is not very much interested in her.

Already seated in the dining room, she is looking down to the beach, where she sees a few runners near the edge of the waves, and a bunch of dogs, of various colors and sizes, that have gathered there at a small outcropping of rocks, as though deciding something. A conference of dogs.

There used to be a lot of cats wandering about the dining room at mealtimes—though careful to keep out of the way of the quick-footed young maids and especially of Oscar, an unpleasant Russian, the manager of the hotel. Evelyn Fisk used to like giving the cats bits of bacon at breakfast, and pieces of meat, or fish, whatever, at night. She was in fact extremely fond of those cats.

Observing that Oscar has just come into the room on some errand, she frowns to herself, and hopes that he won't come over to speak to her.

It must have been Oscar who in some way got rid of the cats.

Oscar, of White Russian parents, is in his own view an aristocrat. No one much likes him. He is erroneously described as a Communist by certain guests; educated in Germany, he is labeled "that Nazi" by another sort of guest. He is very thin and sun-withered, inattentive except for occasional fits of concentrated and usually inappropriate emotion, often rage. He gives an impression of disliking all of Mexico, including the hotel and its guests.

For several years there was a Polish woman of a certain age, named Marya, always there with Oscar and assumed to be his wife. A lean, faded blonde, who simply seems to be no longer around, and no one has asked about her.

Oscar himself does not appear to know who is there from one year to the next, and he has been known to greet an already tanned mid-stay guest as though that person were a new arrival. Today he speaks to no one but a certain maid, who has done some wrong. Oscar scolds her at length, very sharply. He shakes one long finger much too close to her face, so that the girl shrinks and cowers.

"Oh, there's the woman who used to feed the cats," Zelda says to Abe as they settle into their stiff, uncomfortable chairs and look about the room.

"She must miss them." Abe and Zelda have two dogs at home, whom Abe secretly misses very much. He would like to have children, but Zelda postpones even discussions of this possibility with vague remarks about how young they are (how young she is), plenty of time.

"She doesn't look to me as though she missed anyone, or anything," Zelda tells him. "Do you suppose she's married, or what?"

"If she were married, she wouldn't always come here alone, would she?" Logical Abe is often wrong.

"Oh, she might." Zelda does not take trips alone, although

she has thought that she would like to, especially now, with the presence of a lover in her life. In Toronto for the last few years she has managed a travel agency—no reason for her not to travel now. "I miss the cats a lot," she says to Abe. "And there's horrible Oscar. I wonder whatever happened to Marya?"

No newsboys come into the dining room that morning. Possibly they will be down on the beach later on.

Now, in midwinter, and because this bay is surrounded by high mountains, a range extending almost to Mexico City, the sun comes up late and slowly above the eastern ridge, a yellow haze, shafts of light that at last reach the sea.

By midmorning, though, beachtime, the sunlight is well established: heavy, powerful, almost overwhelming. The hotel guests sit beneath their thatched *palapas,* shielded and sunblocked, emerging occasionally to walk toward or run into the sea. To move through waves, in the warm-cool caressing water.

On this particular day the waves are higher than usual, the undertow strong. Good swimmers, like Abe Hoskins, treat the water with some respect, gauging the sizes of waves, waiting before diving through. Deciding not to bodysurf that day.

Abe thinks he read about an odd, unusual conjunction of planets taking place just now, along with a full moon. All that would surely affect the tides?

Looking at the sky, at the unfamiliar thickening gray banks of clouds, Abe thinks that indeed it could rain. Even if it never does.

Zelda is up in their room putting the final touches to their unpacking. Or maybe talking to the room maid, by now an old friend.

Abe wishes he had a Mexico City *News,* the only available
English-language paper.

And he wonders about Gabino.

Evelyn Fisk, several *palapas* away from that of Abe Hoskins,
also wishes for a newspaper, but her wish is mild, and she
manages to content herself for the moment with her thick
paperback, a new Iris Murdoch.

On this first day, though, her attention wanders. In particular, her eye is caught by the vendors who trudge slowly up
and down, barefoot, on the hot white sand. Selling their
awful wares. It seems to Evelyn that this year their faces are
longer and sadder than usual, which could well be the case,
the Mexican economy being what it is: splendid for tourists, over two thousand pesos to the almighty dollar—and
dreadful, punitive for Mexicans, especially of course for the
poor.

Evelyn notices—or, rather, she thinks of something new
today, which is that the women's wares are generally much
better than the men's, and she ponders this fact: vending is
women's work, finally? (This might be something to include
in a letter to Grantly; on the other hand, perhaps not. Grantly's "liberalism," of a somewhat old-fashioned sort, does not
seem to extend itself to feminist issues.)

The shabbiest, saddest-looking vendors of all are those who
sell peanuts. All men, mostly old. The younger and relatively
more prosperous men have terrible carved birds for sale. Or,
so unappealing in this heat, woven woolen rugs.

Many of the women wear a sort of costume: full dark blue
skirts with layers of petticoats, and modestly ample white
blouses with long sleeves and big floppy lace collars. Perhaps
an Indian tribe? They are selling jewelry: armloads of colored

glass or plastic beads, all in lovely colors, dark blues and greens, pinks and amethysts.

And silver, endless streams of silver. Necklaces, bracelets, earrings.

Later, Evelyn will buy presents for all her daughters and her daughters-in-law. Her female grandchildren.

Zelda Hoskins is neither talking to the maid nor unpacking, but writing a secret letter. One that she has written quite often before, and sometimes mailed but more often not. A letter in which she tells her lover, Evan, that they simply must break off. Seeing him makes her feel too terribly guilty with Abe, who after all is so *nice*. No more Evan, never again.

Evan is a computer salesman based in New York who occasionally comes to Toronto, to stay in the Harborfront Hotel, where Zelda has her travel office. These letters of hers never seem to affect him in the slightest; he shows up anyway, no more or less frequently than before. Looking shy, he comes into her office, saying couldn't they at least have a drink in the bar? Maybe lunch? And there they soon are, back in bed again. In love.

Evan does not look at all the part that he plays with Zelda. A worried, chronically rumpled young man, light-skinned (well, sallow) and too thin, he looks more like the other things that he is, a husband and father, with a heavy mortgage in Douglas, Long Island. A salesman. With Zelda, though, as he has often told her, he is someone else, a strong, confident, often laughing man. "Lord, I even feel handsome," he once half-jokingly confided.

"Darling, you are" was of course what Zelda said (with the odd thought that actually of the two men Abe is better-looking, just a little older).

However, today she is not getting far with her letter. "My darling," she has written. And then she is distracted by a rustle of large black birds, just settling in the bush beyond her terrace. Three of them, a family. Their sleek wings shine, with hints of darkest blue, blue-black velvet. "This time I absolutely," Zelda writes before crumpling up her paper.

Abe too has been watching the vendors, and he, like Evelyn Fisk, sees the peanut vendors as the saddest of all. Even their voices are sad, and their faces are so long. Trickle-down economics, Abe thinks. Poverty trickles down very fast to these poorest of the poor.

Just then, though, a group of small boys appears, bearing newspapers. Abe watches as Evelyn (whom he thinks of as the cat woman) buys a paper. But when the boy reaches him, Abe waves him off, saying, "No, Gabino." Meaning, I'm waiting to buy a paper from Gabino.

The child looks puzzled, whether as to Abe's meaning or the identity of Gabino, Abe can't tell, and so he asks, "Gabino. *Dónde?*" (He does know a very few words of Spanish.)

The small boy shrugs and goes off, leaving Abe with no paper. With nothing.

He probably should have bought one, what the hell? A few pesos here or there won't mean much even to Gabino. However, to the next boy with a bunch of papers who cries "English language! Mexico City *News*!" Abe hears himself repeating, "No, Gabino."

This child, though, seems to understand. And he speaks some English. He asks Abe, "You wait Gabino?"

"*Sí!*" Enthusiastically. And then, "Gabino. *Dónde?*"

The small brown monkey face scrutinizes Abe's much larger, paler face before he says, "*Gabino está muerto.* Dead."

"*No.*"

The devil-child begins to laugh. "*Sí, Gabino está muerto!*" and he runs off after the others, down the beach.

There in the heavy heat Abe sits frozen, immobilized. *Muerto.* Does it mean just dead, or killed? Slain, murdered. How awful for there to be just the one word. And how plausible a violent end would be for Gabino, an artful, ambitious little boy, a Mexican street child. It is entirely horrible. Abe has no words, no way of dealing with this.

And should he tell Zelda? Such a shadow over their trip, and Zelda tends to be superstitious.

Easy enough not to tell her, Abe decides.

Perhaps she will buy all her silver presents today, thinks Evelyn Fisk. Get it over with and simply not consider presents again. She decides this as a very young, dark, Indian-looking girl approaches her *palapa,* a girl with lovely, luminous black eyes and terrible teeth, too large for her face, askew, protuberant. But a radiant smile.

Evelyn, whose Spanish is excellent, asks her name.

Lupe.

Evelyn. Eva.

Lupe has a small brown briefcase of silver things, plus the pretty glass necklaces held over her arm. In a random way Evelyn begins to choose. Later she will sort them out, considering their recipients. In the meantime she talks to Lupe.

Is this her first year on the beach selling silver? Evelyn does not believe she has seen her before.

No, Lupe came before with her mother, Carmelita. However, at that time she was still in school for much of the day. Next year Lupe will have for sale tapes, instead of these, and in a deprecating way she indicates her jewels.

Tapes? Evelyn at first does not understand.

Tapes! Music! All kinds of music. All the latest hits. Music, on tapes.

Zelda, passing the *palapa* of Evelyn Fisk to get to her own, to reach Abe, sees Lupe there with her silver, her bright glass, and on an impulse she stops. She smiles, and by way of greeting to Evelyn she says, "Oh, it's all so pretty."

"I'm afraid I've been very extravagant." Evelyn Fisk smiles back. "But I have all these grandchildren. Not to mention daughters."

"Oh, then you are married." Zelda had not meant to say this. The words rushed out, unbidden.

"Oh indeed. Very much so. But I need a little time off, now and then."

"Oh, *really.*"

"Lupe has been telling me that next year she'll have tapes for sale," Evelyn Fisk says firmly, putting an end to further personal conversation.

"You must miss the cats this year," persists Zelda. Her curiosity has been intensely aroused by this woman, whom she sees close up to be much more interesting-looking than from a distance. For one thing, the white pants, dark shirt, and straw hat that across the dining room look like everyone else's clothes are actually extremely smart. Unusual. Working within a hotel has taught Zelda something about such distinctions. She knows at a glance which guests at the Harborfront are rich, or European, or from the States, as opposed to Canadians, rich or medium rich, from Ottawa or Calgary. Evelyn Fisk is very rich, and from the States.

"I try not to think about the cats," says Evelyn Fisk somewhat dismissingly, turning back to Lupe.

. . .

Abe, out in the water, has observed Zelda's arrival at the beach, and he has noted with some surprise her stop at the cat woman's *palapa*. He waves, but she probably can't see him, can't tell him from any other bather out there in the surf. Nearsighted Zelda is vain about her large dark blue eyes: no glasses. He watches as she settles down with her magazines and lotions in their own *palapa,* and he thinks, What a pretty woman. He decides again not to mention Gabino.

The quality of that water, in that particular bay, is amazing, extraordinary. Abe concentrates on his sense of the water, its lively, active buoyancy, its blue-green clearness. Its perfectly embracing warmth. It is quite unlike any other water, Abe believes. A unique experience of water.

Up on the beach, Zelda is talking to a young Mexican. A news vendor, but considerably taller than the rest. Abe watches as she buys a paper from this boy. She seems in fact to engage him quite unnecessarily in some sort of conversation; even at this distance, out in the waves, Abe sees them laugh, notes their friendly postures. And he experiences a flush of jealous blood—so ridiculous, a Mexican child. Still, there have been times with Zelda when she has given him good cause for jealousy. If not actual, at least approximate.

With a jaunty wave to Zelda, the boy heads down the beach with his armload of papers, and after a calculated minute or two Abe starts in. Swimming, not riding waves. Until he stands up and begins to wade.

He can see Zelda, now smiling and waving in his direction. It is probably the stripes on his new bathing suit that she recognizes.

. . .

What Evelyn Fisk absolutely must not think about, she now reminds herself, is just how Oscar got rid of the cats. No speculations along those lines. *None.* Never.

There were quite a lot of cats. Several families.

Oscar must have—

Someone must have—

NO.

"Well, of course it was Gabino," insists Zelda, at lunch, over Abe's continuing incredulity. "I told you, he wanted to thank you for the shoes. Only he's outgrown them and he'd like another pair." She laughs. "Some con man, that kid. I'm sure he'll go far."

"I can't get over hearing *muerto,*" Abe tells her. "It just seemed so plausible for a kid like Gabino. For really any Mexican kid, these days."

"But it wasn't true," Zelda reminds him. "I keep telling you, he's fine. Just suddenly looking adolescent, not a cute little boy anymore. With acne, poor guy."

Abe can less easily imagine Gabino with acne than he was able to imagine him dead.

"Some nerve he has demanding more shoes." Zelda laughs. And she says again, "He'll go far."

"It seems to me that the prawns were better here last year, don't you think?" Abe recognizes his own reluctance to talk about Gabino as he says this. As Zelda sometimes points out, he tends to avoid issues. A male characteristic, according to Zelda.

She now regards him somewhat narrowly, but she seems willing to leave the topic of Gabino. "Maybe," she says of the prawns. "I don't know, it's all still so beautiful here. I don't much notice flaws."

"On the other hand," says Abe, somewhat later in their meal, "why blame Gabino for trying to get anything he can? Lord knows what his life is like. Where he lives. In what. I may send him three more pairs of shoes. Why in hell not?"

By midafternoon, which is still beachtime for most people, between lunch and their long siestas, the color of the sky is a queer bright ocher, unnaturally intense. And the heavy hot still air is rippled by occasional small spasmodic winds. Out at sea, the color is dark and strange.

No one knows what will happen next.

Many guests start up toward their rooms.

Finding themselves together on the path, Evelyn Fisk and Zelda and Abe all smile, murmuring at the oddity of the weather. Abe insists on carrying Evelyn's rather large book bag—at which they exchange a small laugh.

Pausing for a moment—the path is fairly steep—they turn, the three of them simultaneously, for a backward look at the menacing sky, the beach.

And down there beside the water is Oscar, striding along as though rain were out of the question, were expressly forbidden by himself.

Evelyn. "He really is dreadful."

Zelda. "Horrible. I wonder whatever happened to his wife. Remember Marya?"

"Yes, actually I do. Well, it's not hard to cast him as a sort of Bluebeard."

Perhaps from some automatic impulse of male solidarity (women tend to go too far, almost always), Abe demurs. "Well, come on now. But he is a mean S.O.B., that's for sure."

At the top of the path he hands Evelyn her books, they separate and go off to their own rooms, to bed.

And then the rains begin. A heavy roar of water, pounding down. Water slapping against the concrete walkways. Attacking the roof like bullets. A ferocious rain, that goes on and on, and on.

Believing Abe to be asleep, Zelda pulls the light blanket from the end of the bed to cover his shoulders and her own. And then, that small wifely task completed, she burrows down, breathing the unexpectedly new cool air. For her the sounds of rain are a summer sound, any winter rains in Toronto being muffled by snow. But of course it is summer down here, a perpetual summer. That's why they come here.

Zelda then begins to think of a small trip alone somewhere. Maybe to San Francisco. Well, why not? This is something that women do all the time these days. She could get tickets through the agency, and she could see the city, San Francisco! (She notes with some interest that she is not thinking of New York, or Evan.)

Dozing off, Zelda dreams of freedom. Somewhere else.

Beside her, Abe, who is not asleep, is thinking somewhat resentfully of Gabino, who after all could have written a note when he got the shoes. Abe very carefully included his own name and address, both inside and outside the package. A postcard, any sort of acknowledgment would have done. And today he didn't even wait for Abe to come up from swimming. Surely Zelda would have said that that was where he was.

Or would she?

The intensity of the downpour, the extreme heaviness of that deluge suggests that it won't last long, the rainstorm.

But it seems to go on and on, heavy water pouring from the sky.

It could cause some very bad flooding, Abe thinks next, as he envisions the dry riverbeds, the eroded sloping fields that they pass on their way from the airport to this hotel. And in his mind he can also see a cluster of shacks, the floorless dwellings of the very poor. Small and fragile, hardly shelters at all, precariously perched on the crumbling hillside earth.

Where Gabino might well come from.

His resentment vanished as though washed away in the rain, Abe determines that tomorrow he will go and find Gabino. He will find out just where he lives (he has kept the address), what the circumstances of his family are.

Evelyn Fisk, alone in her wide lumpy hard bed, is thinking that if the cats were still around she would at this moment be worried about where they were now, in the drenching, unaccustomed rain. However, she derives small solace from the fact that there are no cats for her to worry about. Really no solace at all.

In a terrible and permanent way she misses all of them, with their long skinny graceful bodies, their blue-green-yellow wise watchful eyes.

Unspeakable Oscar.

And Grantly, never allowing cats in their house. She has never seen him sneeze or turn red, no true allergic symptoms. He simply doesn't like them.

Well, thinks Evelyn, warm beneath her covers, taking in cool air, Well, there's more than one solution to that problem.

And she smiles.

CHILD'S PLAY

A long time ago, in the thirties, two little girls found almost perfect complements in each other. Theirs was a balanced, exceptionally happy friendship: skinny, scared, precocious Prudence Jamieson and pretty, placid, trustful Laura Lee Matthews. Such friendships quite often occur, of course, among small girls. They find each other. What was perhaps unusual about this one was its having been arranged, indeed contrived, by the parents involved, for their own convenience—so often under such circumstances the children refuse to like each other. But Prudence and Laura Lee really took to each other, as their grateful, hard-drinking parents remarked, making everything easy for the parents (for a while).

In any case, in the long, Southern summer twilights, after supper the small girls used to play in the sprawling, bountiful Matthews garden, and one of their favorite pastimes involved making a series of precariously fragile, momentarily lovely dolls out of flower petals. Pansy faces with hollyhock skirts, like dancers' tutus, for example, or petunia skirts and tiny rosebud faces. The idea had been Prudence's, but Laura Lee was more successful in its execution, being more patient and much more deftly fingered. This occupation entirely absorbed both children, and it formed an idyllic part of their childhood, something they lightly, laughingly mentioned to each other as they became more complex but still firm adult friends.

The friendship among the four grown-ups, which did not end well, was based largely upon their shared enthusiasm for drink—three of those four people were borderline alcoholics; the fourth, Sophia Jamieson, mother of Prudence, became a full-fledged alcoholic. Another bond, even more perilous, was the violently flaring, illicit (though never even nearly consummated) love affair between Dan Jamieson, father of Prudence, and Liza Matthews, the beautiful mother of pretty Laura Lee. Given all these danger-fraught circumstances, it is surprising that the four-way adult connection continued for as long as it did; in recent, more accelerated times, disaster might well have struck much sooner.

All these things happened, then, in a place called Hilton, a college town in the middle South, a pleasantly heterogeneous collection of old buildings, old houses, and a lot of ancient brick and ivy and Virginia creeper. Both town and college were built among gently rising inland hills whose green velvet undulations gave credence to a local theory that all that land had once lain beneath the sea.

Many of the faculty members and a few of the more imaginative townspeople lived a mile or so from town in what had once been farmhouses, old rambling structures now more or less converted into practical houses. The Jamiesons, Dan and Sophia and Prudence, lived in one such house on a hilltop; Liza and Carlton Matthews, with Laura Lee, lived on another hill, about a mile away. Small, handsome, jokey Dan Jamieson taught history at Hilton. Big, serious Carlton Matthews was a doctor, one of the two in town, and consequently he was over-worked and often terribly tired; at night he liked to drink. Liza Matthews, in addition to keeping a perfect house and cooking well (and being very beautiful, a blue-eyed, black-haired sprite), was a gifted gardener; almost single-handedly she had achieved the generous garden in which the little girls played their games of dolls among the flowers.

Sophia Jamieson seemed to drink less than the others did, at first; she even carried glasses of Coke and water, resembling bourbon and branch, to fend off assiduous hosts. She was a difficult, complicated woman; to her daughter she was terri-fying. In fact, Prudence was so afraid of her mother that she could not have named that emotion, fear, in much the same way that extremely lonely people often do not quite know that loneliness is what is wrong.

Sophia did not look like a frightening woman. She was small, much smaller than Prudence eventually grew to be, very erect, and somewhat plump, with an oddly unindented body. Long brown hair worn braided, impeccably, around her head. Her skin was reddish brown, often flushed, rather coarsely textured (to Prudence as a small child, those pores seemed amazingly large—frightening holes). Sophia's voice was soft and very gentle (usually); on the whole a quiet person, her presence still was felt in any room—Dan always felt it, as God knows Prudence did. An extremely intelligent, highly efficient woman, Sophia headed the local Red Cross, organiz-ing volunteers and fund drives. Doing good.

Both families had swimming pools, which in those days were not overwhelmingly expensive. The Jamieson pool was down in a ravine, separated from the house by a long, wooded slope (dogwood, maples, small pines). The water in its narrow oval was often cold. The Matthews pool, near their garden, was large and round and shallow, open to sunlight. Warm. (The symbolism of the two pools struck Prudence as an adult, naturally; it was not something mentioned at the time, though others must have thought of it, especially infatuated Dan.) In any case, while the couples still were friends, the Matthews pool was mostly used for daytime swimming; Liza would bring out trays of sandwiches and iced tea or lemonade—none of them were really daylight drinkers.

The Jamieson pool was ideal for summer-night parties. Sophia's maid would leave bowls of potato salad in the icebox, and at suppertime Dan would build a fire down by the pool; he would roast hot dogs, hamburgers, or cube steaks and pass them out in buns to everyone there, the dozen or so good friends. They would all be sitting around on steamer rugs, on the summer dew-damp ground, as fireflies drifted through the darkening evening air. As flirtations and arguments grew heavier with drink.

It was most often Prudence who spent the night at the Matthews house, far out of the way of the parties. Which, for every reason, Prudence loved. Before her parents got to be friends with the Matthewses and she was invited to go spend the night with Laura Lee, the sounds of those poolside parties used to scare her badly. They sang a lot, her parents and their friends, as the night wore on; to Prudence they sounded like the cannibals in Tarzan movies—terrifying! At the Matthewses', she felt safe: there was Laura Lee in the other ruffled white twin bed, and the only night sounds were perfectly ordinary ones: a friendly wind in the trees, someone's dog.

Even the trees around Laura Lee's house seemed safe: sturdy, fat, upright cedars, and nice, small, squat pines.

· · ·

On weekends, the children often took picnics out into the woods that surrounded both their houses. There Prudence was the more adventurous of the two; perhaps being taller gave her more confidence, or maybe it was only people that she feared. She led Laura Lee down a steep hill all billowing with new green leaves, in the springtime, and across a dark field of dry, pale, broken straw, over tiny wildflowers, almost invisible. They pushed through strong, dense, fragrant thickets of honeysuckle and brambles to the stream, where it was Prudence's idea that they should build a dam. And she had a plan, an engineering outline: first stones, then small, thick sticks, and then the whole all packed with mud.

"But, Prudy, we'll get mud all over." Tidy, sweet-faced Laura Lee still laughed as she said this, excited by the very possibility of so much dirt, of such abandon.

"They won't know. We'll sneak home after they've started their cocktails and highballs."

They built the dam—in the course of spring and summer they built a lot of dams, and they came home very dirty, and none of their parents ever minded, really. The children were happy and occupied; they were out of everyone's hair, as the phrase went—and that was the whole point of their knowing each other, wasn't it?

Many people were surprised that Liza Matthews—such a beautiful young woman—should also be so extremely shy. Those who knew something of her background attributed her shyness to that: an isolated, dirt-poor farm in the western, mountainous part of the state, a scholarship to Hilton, waitress jobs. And it is true that Liza felt insecure, always, with people from what she considered to be "good families." (In the South, of course, there is always a lot of such talk, such distinctions.)

Liza was impressed that Carlton was a doctor, and for the most part she liked being married to him; as a wife and mother, she was generally happy and very busy. She was still shy around most other people, however, until they began to be friends with the Jamiesons and Dan introduced her to gin. Before that she had only tasted bourbon, which she hated, and beer—even worse. She had thought she just plain did not like to drink, and Carlton's drinking made her sad; he would drink a lot of beer and fall asleep, very early.

But "You just try this for size, Miss Liza," said dapper, blond, green-eyed Dan Jamieson. "All ladies love pink ladies, I guarantee you." And he handed her something pink and frothy and sweet, on an April night, down by the Jamieson pool. White dogwood bloomed all along the slope of woods leading up to the house, and around the pool a high privet hedge also bloomed, sweet-smelling. The shining, slipping surface of the pool reflected, in its wavering black, stars and a thin white moon.

No one had ever called Liza "Miss Liza" before, and Liza suddenly (crazily!) wished that she were a child, so that she could rush over to Dan and kiss him, like a very polite, very well brought up little girl. Little Miss Liza.

She liked the pink lady, and she began to like the party very much. It was such a beautiful, soft night, so warm for April. The sky was so starry, so richly thick with stars, and that sickle moon, and everyone there was so nice, such good, friendly people, everyone liking her, smiling. Carlton whispered that she was the prettiest woman at the party and, looking around her, Liza saw that this was true. She was the prettiest, and everyone knew that she was pretty—especially Dan Jamieson, who later brought out his accordion and sang some songs, mostly looking at Liza. "Oh carry my loved one home safely to me. . . ."

. . .

A few weeks later, Liza got up her nerve and asked everyone to a party at her house. Carlton bought some gin, and Liza made her special chicken salad and honey rolls, and their party was a big success. Everyone said what a lovely house, a good dinner, and how pretty Liza looked. "She can cook, too," said Dan Jamieson, laughing at Liza.

Friends. It was wonderful to have friends like the Jamiesons, at last. Even their little girls seemed to like each other, to like staying over at each other's house.

Everyone gave parties, and they all drank a lot—everyone but Sophia Jamieson, who seemed pretty straitlaced. With lots of friends, all drinking, though, it seemed all right to Liza to say almost anything at all, and she even told a couple of stories about when she was a little girl and they were all so poor: she and her two older sisters had just one good dress between them, so one time they decided they would all go to the dance for an hour apiece. After her hour, the one in the dress had to come home and let one of the others change into it. Fortunately, the three of them looked a lot alike, and the lights were turned down low in the Legion Hall, where the dance was, so no one knew.

Everyone laughed at the story, even Sophia. "You're a natural storyteller, Miss Liza," Dan Jamieson said, adding in his funny way, "too."

A couple of the other women in town invited Liza to join them at Eubanks, the local drugstore, for Cokes: "Any morning about eleven, after you're done with your marketing." Uncertain, Liza got a little too dressed up the first time she went, but it was all right; they all said how pretty she looked. A woman called Popsie said she had never seen such a pretty dress. And Liza had fun, although she did think a pink lady would have been more fun than just a Coke. The other women, especially that Popsie, all laughed and talked a lot. And when Sophia's name came up (Popsie: "*She* never comes for Cokes, *she's* too busy"), Liza was relieved to hear the edge of malice in their voices, a little of the uneasiness regarding Sophia that she herself felt.

Liza did not understand Sophia at all. Sophia reminded her of a teacher, especially one of the strict ones who might hit your knuckles with her ruler. And with such a handsome, flirty husband, why didn't Sophia fix herself up, just a little bit? Her face was always so red and shiny; could she be so old-timey that she thought face powder was bad?

Liza never spent any time with Sophia, and although she surely did not want to, she felt that their not being friends was odd. From what she had observed and understood of couple friendships, usually the two women would get together between the parties to talk things over; the strongest friendship is between those two, usually—the husbands make nervous jokes about "the girls." But with them, the Jamiesons and Matthewses, it was she and Dan holding everything together.

And the children, Laura Lee and thin little Prudence, Prudy. A strange child; if she were mine, I'd worry about that girl, Liza thought. So skinny and nervous, sometimes she looked to be scared of her own shadow. But at other times she could get very fresh and talk back to grown-ups; in fact, at those times she sounded like Sophia, the same long-worded, show-off way of talking. Only when Prudy came over to stay with Laura Lee did she act like just a plain old little girl.

But didn't Sophia care about the way her husband carried on at parties? Did Sophia somehow think that Dan Jamieson didn't really mean it? Was Dan afraid of Sophia?

In any case, they were never alone together, she and Dan,

not for five minutes—not ever, although it would have been so easy, Liza thought. There she was, at home so much of the day, Carlton off at the hospital or his office, and Laura Lee like as not over at Dan's own house. Dan could just . . . drop in, some afternoon. With no excuse at all. They could (Oh Lord!) kiss, the way she used to do back home with the boys who came over to see her.

Sometimes when they were all down at the pool, Sophia would go back up to her house to go to bed; everyone knew she worked very hard all day, but often she would not even say good night, not to anyone. Liza could never decide whether that made it better or worse, her sneaking out like that. When Sophia did say good night, after she left there would be a guilty lull in the conversation. But it was almost the same when she didn't say good night; eventually, someone would say, "Oh, Sophia must have gone on up to the house," and the same lull would come, as though Sophia questioned their right to be down there carousing—until everyone had had a few more drinks and Dan had picked up the accordion again.

One night in October, during a strange heat wave—hot days like summer coming back again—there was a party at the Jamiesons', but at the last minute Carlton had an emergency at the hospital. The little girls were already upstairs, starting their evening of giggling and whispers, and Liza was almost dressed, when she had to call the Jamiesons to say they couldn't come. But Sophia, who answered the phone, insisted that Liza come by herself. Liza could drop Carlton off at the hospital, which was not too far from the Jamiesons'; he could get a ride over later. Sophia had it all figured out.

The night was almost as hot as the day had been and heavy, starless, purely dark. Liza had on an old dress from the summer before, but it hardly mattered what she wore; no one could see a thing.

That night, Dan didn't play the accordion, because another man, someone's houseguest, was there with his guitar. He was good; he knew some Mexican songs, as well as the old ones they were all so used to. In fact, Liza was so moved by this man's music, so interested, that for a minute she didn't realize that in the darkness Dan had somehow moved over to her steamer rug, where she was sitting all by herself, at the back of the group. But, of course, it was Dan she had been thinking about as she listened to those songs. And now there he was, seated right next to her. His face was just visible, his bright teeth, his smile.

His hand touched hers, then covered it. Slowly, like someone hypnotized, Liza turned her palm upward in his grasp, so that all the naked flesh of their two hands lay tightly together. Liza felt as though all the nerves of her body had moved to that one hand, her hand pushing upward to Dan's pushing downward. Oh, Dan, I love you, I love you so deeply, with everything! cried out Liza, within her heart.

The effects of strong drink on that particular group were interesting in their variety; Prudence, saved from drinking by an ulcer, was later to make this observation. Heavy, tired Carlton passed out early; lively Dan, and probably Liza too, could have stayed up all night, getting drunker and wilder. And then there was lonely, hostile Sophia, who preferred to drink alone.

Another, much earlier observation of Prudence's was that she could get along with either parent alone; two people is all right, she thought. It was the three of them that she found unbearable: the meals full of heavy silences, of too strong emotions. But the three of them were all right with guests around, preferably lots of guests, a party. It was like a geometry theorem in which the triangle is the villain. (She never even considered the possibility of Sophia and Dan alone, partly because they almost never were.)

In any case, during the November week that Dan Jamieson and Carlton Matthews and a couple of other men went duck hunting in the eastern, marshy part of the state, Prudence and Sophia even enjoyed being together, for a while. Sophia talked much more than usual to her daughter, and Prudence experienced an odd elation, quite unfamiliar; at dinner her mother talked about her college days, up North at Bryn Mawr, her studies there in history and economics. ("No one thought those fit subjects for a girl, back then," said Sophia, enjoying her recollected defiance.) Sophia talked about her friends from that time, many of whom she kept in touch with, though still she missed them.

"I think I might like to be a physicist," said Prudence boldly; she was not at all sure what that was, but she hoped the word might appeal to her mother.

"Well, that's a hard profession for a woman to get into. But, Prudence, dear, we know that you're exceptionally intelligent."

Prudence thrilled to her mother's praise and to the attention.

Sophia too seemed to enjoy their time together. "Well, I think I'll have a little sherry with my dessert," she said on a couple of nights. "No reason not to." Gay, liberated Sophia.

And then one night, about an hour after dinner, when Prudence had gone up to her room to do homework and Sophia to her room for whatever she did at night, Prudence heard a loud, determined knock at the front door. And a few minutes later, she heard Sophia's steps going down the front stairs.

It was Liza Matthews. Very surprising: at first, Prudence felt a small chill of fear at the sheer unusualness of Liza's coming to call, and at this hour. But soon she was reassured by the entirely usual sounds of social pleasure she heard from both women down below. Liza explained that she had just been driving by and thought she would drop in for a minute. Sophia expressed joy that Liza should have done so. Drinks were offered and accepted.

Bored with her homework and not quite sleepy yet, Prudence decided to go and listen more closely; her bedroom's situation near the top of the stairs made this easy. She and Laura Lee often sat there listening to parties.

As she settled down, her nightgown tucked up under her knees, Prudence heard Liza announce, "I just have to tell you, Sophia, what I've been thinking and wondering about." Her voice was slurred, but Liza often slurred late at night. "I just wonder how it is," continued Liza, "that you and me, I mean you and I, haven't ever got to be friends."

A silent moment followed, during which ice clinked in glasses.

And then Prudence heard her mother's voice: "That is very possibly because you and me, as you put it, have nothing in common whatsoever."

"Well, I guess—" Liza's voice had begun to tremble a little.

"You guess." Sophia's voice grew louder, and harder. "Well, I know. I know that I have absolutely nothing in common with a low-class little tramp . . . who *drinks.*"

"But Sophia . . ." Was Liza crying now? Very possibly. Prudence herself was trembling on her cold top step.

Sophia made a loud, hoarse sound. Prudence had never heard this noise before, but she knew that it came from her mother.

"Drinks!" Sophia repeated, with emphasis. "Why, Popsie Hooker said you showed up for morning Cokes with gin on your breath."

But her mother sounded drunk too, thought Prudence, her blood chilled, her stomach sick. Even though she could not actually see Sophia's face, she could visualize red-faced Sophia, blinking with rage, could imagine the impotent wringing motion of her hands. Prudence saw and heard the invisible; she recognized her mother's essence.

Liza left, and Prudence went to bed and pretended to sleep.

A few days later, Dan came home, and at breakfast Sophia told him, offhandedly, "Oh, and Liza Matthews came by here one night. Drunk as a skunk, I'm afraid. I wish you could have seen her." Accusative, she stared at her husband.

Prudence too stared at her handsome, duplicitous, frightened father, and she too thought, Oh, I wish you had been here.

But she never, ever described that scene to anyone, not to her father and especially not to Laura Lee, who over the years occasionally would ponder: "You know, Prudy, sometimes I just wonder whatever could have happened between our parents—do you reckon they had some kind of an argument?"

That fall, Liza Matthews was hospitalized with what was said to be pneumonia. Her recovery was long and slow, and at that time the two couples who had been such friends barely saw each other.

The girls saw each other at school now; they were no longer encouraged to ask each other over for the night or for a swim. In fact, both were urged in the direction of other girls, from other families. But at this both children balked: Laura Lee, generally so agreeable, did not want to have Mary Elizabeth over for supper and the night; Prudence would not even go to Henrietta's birthday party.

The next summer, the Jamiesons began a year abroad,

mostly in London—where Prudence was cold and often very lonely, but where she learned so much in school that on coming home she had skipped a grade, which put her a year ahead of Laura Lee.

Still, stubbornly, those two girls stayed friends. Even in high school, when both were taken up with boys and with what had become separate bands of other, peer-group friends, they still spent time together. They would choose, though, curiously, to revert to somewhat childish pursuits together; instead of having a downtown drugstore Coke together as either might have with another friend, Prudence and Laura Lee would take long walks out into the piney woods where once as children they had built their dams and explored. Prudence talked about where she would go to college (somewhere up North), what to study, and, closer to home, what certain boys really meant by what they said. And Laura Lee, who had the same concerns, except that she meant to stay and go to school in Hilton, would listen and offer her own views, but admiringly; she appreciated her friend.

Liza Matthews died young, at forty, of "liver problems." And then, a couple of years after that, Sophia died, of a stroke; at that time it was discovered that she too had been an alcoholic—she left bureaus full of bottles, which she must have meant to clean up sometime. Apparently, when she left all those parties so early, she would then go up to her room and nip at sherry, by herself.

Dan died some years later, of a respectable heart attack, before he could marry the young graduate student who by then was his intended. Carlton Matthews lived the longest of those four, possibly because soon after Liza died he took the cure and never had another drink. But he married another beautiful alcoholic, who also died young. When Carlton died a few years later, he left his house to his daughter, Laura Lee.

Laura Lee married three times, each time a richer man; she had four children, by whom she always seemed quite puzzled, nor could she ever quite understand why her husbands left. Like her mother, she became a pretty alcoholic, at last retiring to Hilton, to her family house, to drink in peace. Prudence, as she had told her mother she would, became a physicist, teaching and working in Chicago, which might or might not have pleased Sophia. Prudence married only once, very early and unhappily but briefly.

The two women, then, remained close friends, not seeing each other often but phoning at crucial moments or just to keep in touch—drunken Laura Lee and terribly sober Prudence, laughing like children. Remembering flower dolls and muddy dams.

FOG

On an unspeakably cold and foggy night one November in San Francisco, something terrible happens to a woman named Antonia Love. She is a painter, middle-aged, recently successful, who has invited some people to her house for dinner (one of whom she has not even met, as yet). But in the course of tearing greens into the salad bowl and simultaneously shooing off one of her cats—the old favorite, who would like to knead on one of her new brown velvet shoes—Antonia, who is fairly tall, loses her balance and falls, skidding on a fragment of watercress and avoiding the cat but landing, *bang,* on the floor, which is Mexican-tiled, blue and white. Hard. Antonia thinks she heard the crack of a bone.

Just lying there for a moment, shocked, Antonia imagines herself a sprawled, stuffed china-headed doll, her limbs all askew, awry. How incredibly stupid, how dumb, she scolds herself; if I didn't want people to dinner, I could just have not asked them. And then: Well, useless to blame myself, there are accidents. The point is, what to do now?

As she tries to move, it is apparent that her left arm indeed is broken; it won't work, and in the effort of trying to move it Antonia experiences an instant of pain so acute that she reels, almost faints, and only does not by the most excruciating effort of will.

The problem of what to do, then, seems almost out of her hands. Since she can't for the moment get up, she also can't call her doctor, nor 911. Nor, certainly, can she go on with making dinner.

Fortunately her coming guests are old close friends (except for the very young man she doesn't know, although he seems to think he has met her somewhere). And, further luck, she is sure that she unlocked the front door, its bell being hard to hear, back here in the kitchen. And so her friends will arrive and they will come on in, calling out to her, and she to them. They will find her ludicrously positioned, they will help— although possibly she is really quite all right, and will manage to get up by herself any minute now.

A new flash of pain as she tries to move convinces Antonia that her arm is really broken, and again she castigates herself for clumsiness, for evident ill will toward her friends, determined self-defeat. For steady progress toward no progress at all—oh, for everything!

In addition to which she has probably scared her cat quite badly. He is nowhere around, although she calls out to him, "Baron! Baron?"

No cat, then, and no live-in lover either, since Reeve is at the moment off on one of his restless trips somewhere; Reeve who in an off-and-on way lives there with Antonia, the arrangement being that both are "free." And just as well he is gone, thinks Antonia; he so hates debility, hates bodily things going wrong. (But in that case why has he chosen to live, more or less, with an "older woman," whose body must inevitably decline?) Antonia wonders if Reeve is alone on this trip (she knows that he sometimes is not), but she finds that she lacks just now the stamina for jealous speculation.

Her arm really hurts badly, though; she wishes someone would come, and she wonders who will be the first—who will come in to find her in this worse than undignified position? Will it be her old friend from school days, Lisa, who is bringing the strange young man? Or will it be Bynum and Phyllis, who are old friends—or Bynum is. He is a sculptor, and Phyllis, his latest wife, a very young lawyer. Antonia believes they are not getting along very well.

Or (at this new notion Antonia grimaces to herself) it could always be tall, thin, sandy Reeve himself, who is given to changing his mind, to turning around and away from trips, and people. Reeve, a painter too, is more apt to come home early from trips on which he is accompanied than from those he takes alone; but even that is not a formulation on which anyone, especially Antonia, should count.

Antonia is aware that her friends wonder why she "puts up" with Reeve, his absences, his occasional flings with young art students. And she considers her private view of him: an exceptional man, of extreme (if occasional) sensitivity, kindness—a painter of the most extraordinary talent. (On the other hand, sometimes she too wonders.)

Antonia knows too that her friends refer to Reeve as "Antonia's cowboy" . . .

Reeve is from Wyoming.

She tries next to lie down, believing that some rest might help, or ease the pain, which now seems to have become a constant. Never mind how appalling the spectacle of herself would be, her oversized body sprawled across the floor. However, she can't get down, can't reach the floor; the broken arm impedes any such changes of position. Antonia finds that the most she can achieve is leaning back against table legs, fortunately a heavy, substantial table.

Perry Loomis, the unmet guest, is a journalist, just getting started, or trying to in New York. He could surely sell an article about such a distinguished, increasingly famous woman, especially since Antonia never gives interviews. Now, having cleverly engineered this meeting, and being driven in from Marin County by Antonia's old friend Lisa, Perry is over-excited, unable not to babble. "It said in *Time* that a lot of speculators are really grabbing up her stuff. Even at thirty or forty thousand per. She must hate all that, but still."

"It's hard to tell how she does feel about it," Lisa responds. "Or anything else, for that matter. I think success has been quite confusing to Antonia."

The bay is heavily fogged, slowing their progress from Mill Valley into town, to Antonia's small house on Telegraph Hill. Not everyone slows, however; an occasional small, smart sports car will zoom from nowhere past Lisa's more practical Ford wagon. Scary, but she does not even think of asking this young man to drive. They met through friends at a recent gallery (not the opening) at which Antonia's work was being shown. Perry described himself as a "tremendous Antonia Love fan" and seemed in his enthusiasm both innocent and appealing. Which led Lisa fatally to say, "Oh, really, I've known her almost all my life." Which was not even quite true, but which, repeated to Antonia, led up to this dinner invitation. "Well, why don't you bring him along when you come next Thursday? I'm almost sure Reeve won't be here, and poor Bynum must be tired of being the token man."

"And she's so beautiful," rattles Perry. "Was she always such a beauty?"

"Well, no," says Lisa, too quickly. "In fact, I don't quite see—but you know how old friends are. As a young woman, she was just so—big. You know, and all that hair."

"But I met her," Perry reminds her firmly. "At that thing in New York. She had on the most marvelous dress, she was ravishing, really."

"Oh yes, her green dress. It is good-looking. I think she paid the earth for it. That's one of the points about darling Antonia, really. Her adorable inconsistencies. A dress like that but never a sign of a maid or even a cleaning person in her house." And just why is she sounding so bitchy? Lisa wonders.

"Maybe she thinks they'd get in her way?" Perry's imagination has a practical turn. As a schoolboy, which was not all that long ago, he too meant to be an artist, and was full of vague, romantic plans. However, during college years, in the late seventies, he came to see that journalism might better serve his needs, a judgment seemingly correct. However, his enthusiasm for "artists," in this instance Antonia, is a vestige of that earlier phase.

"Well, she's in any case a marvelous cook," Lisa promises warmly. And then, somewhat less charitably, "Her cooking is surely one of those things that keeps young Reeve around."

"But isn't he a painter too?" Saying this, with an embarrassed twinge Perry realizes that he has imagined Reeve, described in Antonia Love articles as her "young painter companion" as a slightly older version of himself. He had looked forward to seeing just what of himself he would find in Antonia's Reeve.

"Of course he's a painter, that's nine-tenths of the problem right there. Reeve's from Wyoming, we call him 'Antonia's cowboy.' But they should never—Oh, look. *Damn.* There must be an accident on the bridge. Damn, we'll never get there."

Before them, on the downward, entirely fog-shrouded approach to the Golden Gate Bridge, what now seems heavy traffic is halted, absolutely. Red brake lights flicker as thick cold moisture condenses and drips in rivulets down windshields, windows, as somewhere out in the depthless, dangerous bay the foghorns croak, and mourn.

"Oh dear," says Perry Loomis. Although this attractive, rather interesting "older woman" was kind enough to bring him to his object, the desired Antonia, he thinks he really doesn't like her very much. (Are she and Antonia Love the same age? he wonders. This one looks younger, he thinks.)

"Indeed," says Lisa. On the whole an honest woman, she now admits to herself that she agreed to bring this Perry along not entirely out of kindness; there was also (she confesses to herself) some element of fantasy involved, specifically a romantic fantasy of herself with a younger lover (Lisa has been twice divorced, most recently two years back, from an especially mean-spirited lawyer). And then: Oh God, she thinks. Do I have to spend my life trying to be Antonia?

Reeve, who did indeed start out for Oregon, and alone, has now made a wide detour via the Richmond-San Rafael Bridge and is headed for Berkeley. Where, as Antonia might have guessed, had she the energy, there is a girl, Sharon, in whom Reeve is "interested." At this moment, heading along the foggy freeway toward the Berkeley exits, he longs to talk to Sharon, talking being so far about all they have done.

It's very difficult living with Antonia, he would like to tell Sharon. Here she is so successful, everything people work for, and she doesn't believe it. In her mind she's still starving and probably lonely. I mean, it's very hard to live with someone whom nothing can convince that she's all right. Nothing can convince her that people love her, including me.

Sharon is one of the most beautiful young women that Reeve has ever seen; he rather suspects that she was hired in the Art Department, where she works, on that basis—she was formerly a model. A darkly creamy blonde, with dreamy, thick-lashed blue-green eyes, Sharon holds her perfect body forward like a prize; she moves like a small queen—and she would not understand a single word of all that Reeve would like to say. To Sharon it would all be the ancient complaints about a wife.

In fact, the only person who could make the slightest sense of his ravings is Antonia herself. Reeve, a somewhat sardonic, self-mocking young man, comes to this conclusion with a twisting, interior smile. And, on an impulse, passing Sharon's exit, which is University, and heading toward the fog-ladened Bay Bridge, he speeds up the car.

"Phyllis and Bynum, Lisa. Perry. I'll be back soon. Sorry. Stew and risotto in the oven. Salad and wine in refrig. Please take and eat. Love, Antonia."

This note, taped to Antonia's door, was found by Phyllis and Bynum, one of whose first remarks to each other then was "Who on earth does she mean by Perry?"

"Oh, some new young man of Lisa's, wouldn't you say?"

"But what could have happened to Antonia?"

"One of her meetings, wouldn't you imagine? One of her good works." This last from Bynum, Antonia's oldest friend, who has very little patience with her, generally.

That exchange takes place on the long stairs leading up to

the small, shabby-comfortable living room in which they soon
sit, with glasses of wine, engaged in speculations concerning
their hostess.

"Something could be wrong?" Phyllis ventures. A small,
blond, rather pretty woman, she is much in awe of Antonia,
whom she perceives as exceptionally *strong,* in ways that she,
Phyllis, believes herself not to be.

"I doubt it." Big, gnarled Bynum frowns.

This room's great feature—to some its only virtue—is the
extraordinary view afforded of the city, even now, despite the
thick fog. City lights still are faintly visible, everywhere,
though somewhat muffled, dim, and the looming shapes of
buildings can just be made out against the lighter sky.

Phyllis, who is extremely tired (a grueling day in court; but
is she also tired of Bynum, as she sometimes thinks?), now
lounges across a large, lumpy overstuffed chair, and she sips
at the welcome cool wine. (The very size of Antonia's chair
diminishes her to almost nothing, Phyllis feels.) She says,
"Obviously, the view is why Antonia stays here?"

"Contrariness, I'd say," pontificates Bynum, himself most
contrary by nature. "I doubt if she even notices the view anymore."

A familiar annoyance tightens Phyllis's throat as she mildly
says, "Oh, I'll bet she does." She is thinking, if Bynum and
I split up, I'll be lucky to get a place this nice, he doesn't
have to keep putting it down. This could cost, oh, close to a
thousand.

"Besides, the rent's still so low," continues Bynum, as
though Phyllis had not spoken, perhaps as though he had read
her mind.

A pause ensues.

"God, I'm so hungry," says Phyllis. "Do you think we
should really go ahead with dinner?"

"Baby, I sure do." Bynum too is tired, a long sad day of not being able to work. And he too is hungry. "Antonia could be forever, and Lisa and her young man lost somewhere out in the fog."

The immediate prospect of food, however, serves to appease their hunger. They smile pleasantly at each other, like strangers, or those just met. Phyllis even thinks what a handsome man Bynum is; he looks wonderful for his age. "Was Antonia good-looking back when you first knew her?" she asks him.

"Well, she was odd." Bynum seems to ruminate. "She varied so much. Looking terrific one day, and really bad the next. But she was always, uh, attractive. Men after her. But the thing is, she doesn't know it."

"Oh, not even now?" Phyllis, disliking her own small scale, her blond pallor, admires Antonia's larger, darker style. Antonia is so emphatic, is what Phyllis thinks.

"Especially not now." Bynum's smile and his tone are indulgent.

"Do you remember that really strange thing she said, when she told a reporter, 'I'm not Antonia Love'?" asks Phyllis. She has wanted to mention this before to Bynum, but they have, seemingly, no time for conversation.

"I think she meant that she could only view herself as created," Bynum explains authoritatively.

Phyllis is not sure whether he is speaking as a fellow artist or simply as an old friend. She asks, "Do you mean by the media?" She is aware of enjoying this conversation, perhaps because it is one, a conversation.

"Oh no, so much more sinister," Bynum assures her. "By herself. She thinks she's someone she's painted." He chuckles a little too loudly.

And loses the momentary sympathy of his young wife. Declining to comment, though, and remembering how hungry she is, Phyllis gets up to her feet. "Well, I don't care how lost Lisa and what's-his-name are. I'm heating up dinner."

She goes out into the kitchen as Bynum calls after her, "I'll be there in a minute."

But several minutes pass, during which Bynum does not follow Phyllis. Instead he stares out the window, out into the dark, the enveloping, thickening fog. Into dimmed yellow lights.

He is fairly sure that Phyllis will leave him soon; he knows the signs—the ill-concealed small gestures of impatience, the long speculative looks, the tendencies to argument. How terribly alike they all seem, these girls that he marries. Or is it possible that he sees none of them very sharply, by herself— that he can't differentiate? One of them made this very accusation, referring to what she called his "myopia." In any case, he will probably not miss Phyllis any more than he missed the others, and in a year or so he will find and marry a new young woman who is very much like Phyllis and the rest. He knows that he must be married.

A strong light wind has come up, rattling the windowpanes. Standing there, still looking out, Bynum has a brand-new thought—or, rather, a series of thoughts. He thinks, Why do they always have to be so goddam young? Just who am I kidding? I'm not a young man. A woman of my own age or nearly might at last be a perfect companion for me. A woman artist, even, and he thinks, Well, why not Antonia? This place is a dump, but she's so successful now we could travel a lot. And I've always liked her really, despite our fights. This Reeve person must surely be on the way out. She won't put up with him much longer—so callow.

"Bynum, come on, it's all ready," Phyllis then calls out as at that same instant the doorbell rings.

It is of course Lisa and the new young man, Perry, who looks, Bynum observes, far too smugly pleased with himself.

Introductions are made, warm greetings exchanged: "But you look marvelous! Have you been here long? Yes, I'm sure we met at the gallery. How very like Antonia not to be here. But whatever could have happened?"

"Actually, it is not at all like Antonia not to be here," Bynum announces. He is experiencing a desire to establish himself as the one of them who knows her best.

Over dinner, which indeed is excellent—a succulent veal stew, with a risotto—Bynum scrutinizes Lisa, and what looks to be her new friend. Lisa is looking considerably less happy than the young man is, this Perry, in Bynum's view. Could they possibly have made it in the car, on the way over here, and now Lisa is feeling regrets? Even to Bynum's somewhat primitive imagination this seems unlikely.

What Lisa regrets is simply having talked as much as she did to Perry as on the way over they remained locked in the fogbound traffic. She not only talked, she exaggerated, over-emphasized Antonia's occasional depression, even her worries over Reeve.

And even while going on and on in that way, Lisa was visited by an odd perception, which was that she was really talking about herself. She, Lisa, suffers more than occasional depressions. It is her work, not Antonia's (well, hardly Antonia's), that seems to be going nowhere. And Lisa, with no Reeve or anyone interesting in her life at the moment, is worried that this very attractive young man will not like her (she has always liked small, dark, trimly built men like Perry). Which is really why she said so much about Antonia—gossip as gift, which is something she knows about, having done it far too often.

The truth is—or one truth is—that she is deeply, permanently fond of Antonia. And another truth is that her jealous competitiveness keeps cropping up, like some ugly, uncontrolled weed. She has to face up to it, do something about it, somehow.

"What a superb cook Antonia is," she now says (this is true, but is she atoning?). "Her food is always such a treat."

"The truth is that Antonia does everything quite well," Bynum intones. "Remember that little spate of jewelry design she went into? Therapy, she called it, and she gave it up pretty quickly, but she did some lovely stuff."

"Oh, Bynum," Lisa is unable not to cry out. "How can you even mention that junk? She was so depressed when she did it, and it did not work as therapy. You know perfectly well that she looked dreadful with all those dangles. She's too big."

Perry laughs as she says this, but in a pleasant, rather sympathetic way, so that Lisa thinks that maybe, after all, he understood? understood about love as well as envy?

Below them on the street now are the straining, dissonant, banging sounds of cars: people trying to park, trying to find their houses, to get home to rest. It is hard to separate one sound from another, to distinguish, identify. Thus, steps that must be Antonia's, with whomever she is with, are practically upon them before anyone has time to say, "Oh, that must be Antonia."

It is, though: Antonia, her arm in its bright white muslin sling thrust before her, in a bright new shiny plaster cast. Tall Antonia, looking triumphant, if very pale. And taller Reeve, somewhat disheveled, longish sandy hair all awry, but also in his own way triumphant, smiling. His arm is around Antonia's shoulder, in protective possession.

First exclamations are in reaction to the cast. "Antonia, how terrible! However did you? How lucky that Reeve—How awful, does it still hurt? Your *left* arm, how lucky!"

Reeve pulls out a chair for Antonia, and in an already practiced gesture with her good, lucky right arm she places the cast in her lap. In a somewhat embarrassed way (she has never been fond of center stage), she looks around at her friends. "I'm glad you went on with dinner" is the first thing she says. "Now you can feed us. God, I'm really starving."

"I came home and there she was on the floor—" Reeve begins, apparently about to start a speech.

"The damn cat!" Antonia cries out. "I tripped over Baron. I was making the salad."

Reeve scowls. "It was very scary," he tells everyone present. "Suppose I hadn't come home just then? I could have been traveling somewhere, although—"

This time he is interrupted by Bynum, who reasonably, if unnecessarily, states, "In that case, we would have been the ones to find Antonia. Phyllis and I."

"I do wish someone would just hand me a plate of that stew," Antonia puts in.

"Oh of course, you must be starved," her friends all chorus. "Poor thing!"

It is Lisa who places the full, steaming plate before Antonia, Lisa asking, "You can eat okay? You want me to butter some bread?"

"Dear Lisa. Well, actually I do, I guess. God, I hope I don't get to like this helplessness."

"Here." Lisa passes a thick slice of New York rye, all buttered. "Oh, and this is Perry," she says. "He's been wanting to meet you. You know, we drove down from Marin together."

Antonia and Perry acknowledge each other with smiles and

small murmurs, difficult for Antonia, since she is now eating, ravenously.

"Real bastards in the emergency ward," Reeve is telling everyone; he obviously relishes his part in this rescue. "They let you wait forever," he says.

"Among bleeding people on gurneys," Antonia shudders. "You could die there, and I'm sure some people do, if they're poor enough."

"*Does* it hurt?" asks Lisa.

"Not really. Really not at all. I just feel so clumsy. Clumsier than usual, I mean."

She and Lisa smile at each other: old friends, familiar irony.

Now everyone has taken up forks again and begun to eat, along with Antonia. Wine is poured around, glasses refilled with red, or cold white, from pitchers.

Reeve alone seems not to be eating much, or drinking—for whatever reasons of his own: sheer excitement, possibly, anyone who thinks about it could conclude. He seems nervy, geared up by his—their recent experience.

The atmosphere is generally united, convivial, though. People tell their own accident stories, as they will when anyone has had an accident (hospital visitors like to tell the patient about their own operations). Bynum as a boy broke his right arm not once but twice, both times falling out of trees. Lisa broke her leg on some ice. "You remember, Antonia, that awful winter I lived in New York. Everything terrible happened." Perry almost broke his back, "but just a fractured coccyx, as things turned out," falling off a horse, in New Mexico (this story does not go over very well, somehow; a lack of response can be felt around the room). Phyllis broke her arm skiing in Idaho.

Reeve refrains from such reminiscences—although he is such a tall, very vigorous young man; back in Wyoming, he must have broken something, sometime. He has the air of a man who is waiting for the main event, and who in the meantime chooses to distance himself.

In any case, the conversation rambles on in a pleasant way, and no one is quite prepared to hear Antonia's end-of-meal pronouncement. Leaning back and looking around, she says, "It's odd that it's taken me so long to see how much I hate it here."

This is surely something that she has never said before. However, Antonia has a known predilection for the most extreme, the most emotional statement of any given feeling, and so at first no one pays much serious attention.

Lisa only says, "Well, the city's not at its best in all this fog. And then your poor arm."

And Bynum? "You can't mean this apartment. I've always loved it here." (At which Phyllis gives him a speculative, not quite friendly look.)

Looking at them all—at least she has everyone's attention—Antonia says, "Well, I do mean this apartment. It's so small, and so inconvenient having a studio five blocks away. Not to mention paying for both. Oh, I know I can afford it, but I hate to." She looks over at Reeve, and a smile that everyone can read as significant passes between the two of them.

One of Antonia's cats, the guilty old tabby, Baron, has settled on her lap, and she leans to scratch the bridge of his nose, very gently.

And so it is Reeve who announces, "I've talked Antonia into coming back to Wyoming with me. At least to recuperate." He smiles widely (can he be blushing?), in evident pleasure at this continuation of his rescuer role.

"I'm so excited!" Antonia then bursts out. "The Grand Tetons, imagine! I've always wanted to go there, and somehow I never dared. But Reeve has this whole house, and a barn that's already a studio."

"It's actually in Wilson, which is just south of Jackson," Reeve explains. "Much less touristic. It's my folks' old place."

If Antonia expected enthusiasm from her friends about this project, though, she is disappointed.

Of them all Bynum looks most dejected, his big face sags with displeasure, with thwarted hopes. Phyllis also is displeased, visibly so (but quite possibly it is Bynum of whom she disapproves?).

Lisa cries out, "But, Antonia, what'll I do without you? I'll miss you so, I'm not used to your being away. It'll be like New York—"

To which Antonia smilingly, instantly responds, "You must come visit. Do come, we could start some sort of colony. And, Bynum, you can use this place while I'm gone if you want to."

Perry of course is thinking of his article, of which he now can envision the ending: Antonia Love off to the wilds of Wyoming, putting fogbound, dangerous San Francisco behind her. He likes the sound of it, although he is not quite sure that Jackson or even Wilson would qualify as "wilds." But there must be a way to find out.

In any case, he now sees that he has been quite right in his estimate of Antonia: she is beautiful. At this moment, radiantly pale, in the barely candlelit, dim room, her face is stylized, almost abstract, with her broad, heavy forehead and heavy dark brows, her wide-spaced large black eyes and her wide, dark-painted mouth. It will be easy to describe her: stylized, abstract.

She is of course not at all his type (he actually much prefers her friend Lisa, whom he has decided that he does like, very much; he plans to see her again)—nor does Perry see himself in Reeve, at all. He senses, however, some exceptional connection between the two of them, some heightened rapport, as though, already in Wyoming, they breathed the same heady, pure, exhilarating air.

Antonia is talking about Wyoming now, her imagined refuge. "Mountains, clouds, water. Wildflowers," she is saying, while near her side Reeve smiles, quite privately.

And Perry believes that he has struck on the first sentence of his article: "Antonia Love these days is a very happy woman."

LOST CAT

Her cat is lost. Maggie calls and calls, standing there at the edge of the woods, in misting, just beginning rain. In Inverness, California, Maggie's parents' weekend house.

But the cat is gone, is nowhere. Not answering, invisible for an hour.

And generally sensible Maggie feels that she cannot continue in her life without this cat. Without red-gold Diana, regal Diana, of the long plumy tail and wide, mad yellow eyes. This is the breaking point, the true turning downward of her life, Maggie thinks. It is what she always dimly, darkly knew would happen: Diana gone. No more beautiful cat, whom she never deserved, who was only a visitor in Maggie's life.

Still calling, "Kitty, kitty, Diana"—at the same time Maggie knows that what she is feeling is ludicrous: preposterous to care so much for a cat that you think you will die without her. But Diana is me, Maggie next (and even more crazily) thinks. If Diana is gone, I am gone.

And such thoughts from a woman in the very field of mental health! Maggie is a psychiatric social worker, has had years of therapy; she is steeped in theoretic knowledge of the mind. She spends her days helping others to be a little more sane (or trying to help them), or at least to cope in some way with their given lives.

Behind her the huge house looms, gray-shingled, mullion-windowed. All tidy now and tightly packed for her leaving, as it has been for the past hour. Her clothes and books in their bags, her parents' kitchen immaculate. A big sane house. In that moment, though, the moment of calling out to Diana through the rain, everything that once seemed all right now looks crazy, including the house. Crazy that she, Maggie, an independent (in most ways) young woman, long out on her own, should still seek a lonely weekend refuge in the family stronghold—and should spend at least two hours, as she just now has, in tidying, tightening up the house, as though to leave no trace of her own light passage there. As though she, like Diana, were some light-footed visitor. Temporary. A shadow of a person.

"Diana, Diana, kitty . . ." she calls, sure that no one and especially not Diana, the wily cat, can hear her.

In the meantime the mist has become true rain, gentle rain but very firm, persistent. Maggie's face is wet, and her long hair, her Shetland sweater, her skirt. It's getting dark. Harder and harder to find a willful cat who could have simply strayed off into the woods. Been attacked. Badly hurt. Or simply lost. Gone, for good.

On the other hand, a more sensible, practical Maggie thinks, cats generally come home. If she goes back into the house, maybe makes a cup of tea, Diana will very, very likely emerge, from wherever. She will stroll out nonchalantly, not even especially friendly, not imagining that either scoldings or excessive greetings are in order.

Diana is fifteen now, not remarkably old for a cat, but fairly old; could she have chosen now to go off into the woods to die? In the darkening thickets, tangled bent gray cypresses and tall heavy firs, in the rain?

An outrageous cat, more outrageous even than most cats are. She is sometimes passionately affectionate; she will press her fine-boned body against Maggie's leg, or her shoulder, with purrings and rubbings. But at other times, which are wholly of Diana's choosing, she can be haughty, even cross; she has a large vocabulary of negative sounds, as well as her loud, round purr.

But where—oh, where is she now?

Maggie's chest hurts, and her breath comes hard, and at the same time she is humiliated, deeply shamed by what strikes her as deranged: such an extreme, an "inappropriate" reaction to the loss of a cat, whom she surely must have known would someday die.

Turning from the woods (where Diana is?), Maggie heads slowly back across the tousled pale winter lawn to the house, the enormous house, every inch of which she has searched: under beds, back into closets, under sofas and chairs, behind shelves and more shelves of books.

In the kitchen, her mother's kitchen (now entirely her mother's, so clean, all traces of Maggie removed), with tranced, slow motions Maggie puts on some water for tea as she wonders, Why is it that by this time of her life she does not have a place of her own, other than her very small North Beach rooms, in San Francisco? Because I can't afford to buy anything, or to rent something larger, another familiar, more reasonable voice responds. Because in a quite deliberate way I chose an underpaid field, social work. And have chosen (more or less) not to marry, only to like men somewhat similarly engaged—recently Jonathan, a sculptor. Never lawyers or doctors or men in stock or real estate, *never*.

Pouring tea into her own blue pottery cup, Maggie then sips, and she tries, tries very, very hard, to think in a rational way.

One solution would be to spend the night out here, in Inverness; obviously, the longer she is here, the more time there will be during which Diana could somehow show up. Maggie could redo her bed and get up very early, get back to the city by eight, when she has an appointment with Hue Wan Griggs and his mother, who are always meticulously prompt—coming all the way to the clinic from their Tenderloin (condemned) hotel.

However, at that vision of herself, raw-eyed with sleeplessness and still quite possibly without Diana, Maggie's mood plunges once more downward, blackly, into hopelessness, and she has what is really her most deranged thought so far. She thinks, If Diana does not come back, if I never find her, it means that Jonathan will leave, go back to Boston, and that the next time I have a mammogram they will find something bad, some shadow on the film that means I will die.

Loss of Jonathan and getting cancer are Maggie's most familiar fears, and at worst they seem (if unconsciously) related, try as she will to separate them rationally.

Jonathan: a sculptor who works in a restaurant that he despises, for a living. He too lives in North Beach, in an even smaller, cheaper place than Maggie's. Living together would save them money, they know that; however, they also agree that for them having the two places is much better. Both privacy and a certain freshness are preserved. They can take turns playing host at dinner, enjoying small ceremonies. Or on the nights that they do not spend together (Jonathan often likes to work at night) they will meet for breakfast, fresh hard Italian rolls and morning love.

That is how in good times Maggie and Jonathan "relate" to each other. (The jargon of Maggie's profession, mixed with worse from pop psychology, is ironically used by them both, part of a well-developed private language.) In bad times Jonathan hates San Francisco, along with his job in the silly, pretentious restaurant; and sometimes Maggie feels herself included in his discontent.

Cancer: Maggie's history is "unfortunate." Her mother and two aunts had fairly early mastectomies. However, all three women are still alive and seemingly well: successful surgery. Conscientious (frightened) Maggie has yearly mammograms, and she worries. Especially when Jonathan rails against the city, when he says that he is sure he could find a better job in Boston, or even in New York—then, imagining his departure, Maggie imagines too that in her grief she will also find a lump. And her full awareness of the total irrationality of this view is not much help.

And now—Diana.

Her tea, though, has imparted some hope to Maggie, along with its comforting warmth. Or, having gazed for some moments at the wilds of her own unreason, she feels more reasonable?

In any case, she stands up resolutely, and stretches a little before taking her teacup and saucer over to the sink, neatly washing and drying and putting them away. *Of course* Diana will show up sooner or later, Maggie now thinks. If not tonight, tomorrow. At worst, she, Maggie, could call in sick (a thing she has never once done); Hue Wan and his mother, and her five or six other appointments could get through the day without her. Couldn't they?

Going outside to try calling Diana again, and again, she thinks that now, for sure, Diana will emerge through the trees, with her slightly loose-jointed walk, her mad yellow blinking eyes, in the dark.

At the upward slope of the house a wide path leads to the crest of the hill, from which one can see the ocean—on clear days, the brilliant Pacific. Almost nothing would be visible up there now, in the gathering, thickening dark; still, Maggie has an odd impulse to take that path, to hike up across gullies and fallen trees and rocks to the top of the ridge, to look out at the black space where the sea must be.

However, even for Maggie in her current state of unreason, this seems too extreme a step, and she finds herself thinking instead about Hue Wan Griggs, whom she might or might not see tomorrow. Hue is part Vietnamese, part black, very dark and small for his age, with wide, amazingly beautiful, luminous, heavy-lashed eyes. And diagnosed as autistic—no contact, just hitting, bumping into things, staring off. But last week he smiled, he actually smiled in what Maggie believed was her direction. And now she feels a pang of loss at the thought that she could miss another such smile.

But no Diana. In the light steady rain and the increasing cold, Maggie stands and calls, and calls, and no cat comes. And all her plans and half-decisions seem then to dissolve in that rain. Whether she stays overnight or goes back to the city is wholly unimportant, for nothing will work, she now thinks. Her superstitious wooing of Diana or perhaps of fate itself was to no avail. Of course not.

Sodden-hearted, she turns again toward the house, without a plan. Irrelevantly and painfully she is remembering a weekend that she and Jonathan (and Diana, of course they brought her along) spent at this house last summer, a time that she later came to think of as perfect. Or as close to perfect as imperfect humans can arrive at. (And cats: Diana, a non-hunter, chased mice and squirrels, and lost, but seemed to enjoy the chase.) Perfect soft bright weather for hikes and picnic feasts. Amazingly brilliant views of the sea, and of further piney ridges, cliffs of rocks. Amazing love.

Looking up at the huge square gray house before her, Maggie now sees it as inhabited by shades. By Jonathan, and by her parents. By beautiful, gone Diana.

Reluctantly she opens the front door. She goes into the living room, and there, an orange-gold mound in the middle of the sofa, there is Diana: Diana entirely engrossed in grooming her tail, licking, burrowing for a probably imaginary flea. Not even looking up.

And of course there is no way to find out, ever, where she has been, and much less why: why she should hide for what is now almost three hours, why hide when she must have heard Maggie call, and call, from wherever she was, in however deep a sleep.

An hour or so later, Maggie is driving her small car back across the Golden Gate Bridge, in the murky yellow lights (the supposed suicide-deterrents). Her overnight bag and the small sack of leftover food and her books are on the back seat, and Diana, as always, is sleeping on Maggie's lap; she is simply there, asleep and lightly purring, shedding golden hairs on Maggie's dark, still-damp skirt.

And Maggie can no longer even invest the return of her cat with magic meanings: Jonathan might still decide to throw it all up and move back to Boston, or New York; a mammogram could still hold bad news for Maggie. None of her wildest, her most despairing thoughts are assuaged for good. Tonight when she gets home she will call Jonathan, who may or may not feel like coming over to see her. And tomorrow morning at eight she will meet with small, doe-eyed Hue Wan Griggs, who may or may not smile.

TIDE POOLS

For some years I lived alone in a small white clapboard house, up on a high wooded bluff above the Mississippi River, which I could hardly see—so far down, glimpsed through thick vines and trees, and so narrow just there.

This was near Minneapolis, where I was an assistant professor at a local college. Teaching marine biology. And I thought quite a lot about the irony of my situation—a sea specialty in the landlocked Midwest. (I am from Santa Barbara, California, originally, which may explain quite a bit.)

During those Minnesota years, despite professional busyness, a heavy teaching load, labs, conferences, friends, and a few sporadic love affairs, I was often lonely, an embarrassing condition to which I would never have admitted. Still, and despite my relative isolation, at that time I regarded the telephone as an enemy, its shrill, imperative sound an interruption even to loneliness. When my phone rang, I did not anticipate a friendly chat. For one thing, most of my friends and lovers were also hard-working professionals, not much given to minor social exchange.

Thus, on a summer night about a year ago, a rare warm clear twilight, reminding me of Southern California, I was far from pleased at the sound of the telephone. I had just taken a bath and finished dressing; I was going out to dinner with a man I had met recently, whom I thought I liked. (Was he calling to break the date? Native distrust has not helped my relationships with men, nor with women.) We were going out to celebrate my birthday, actually, but I did not imagine that the ringing phone meant someone calling with congratulations, my birthday not being something that I generally talk about.

What I first heard on picking up that alien instrument was the hollow, whirring sound that meant a long-distance call, and I thought, How odd, what a strange hour for business. Then, as I said hello, and hello again, I heard silence. At last a female voice came on, very slurred. But then words formed. "Judith? Have I got Miss Judith Mallory? *Dr.* Mallory?"

"Yes—"

"Judy, is that you, truly? Truly, Jude? Judy, do you know who this is?" An excited, drunken voice, its cadence ineradicably familiar to me—and only one person has ever called me Jude. It was Jennifer Cartwright, my closest early-childhood friend, my almost inseparable pal—whom I had not heard from or about for more than twenty years, not since we both left Santa Barbara, where we grew up together, or tried to.

I asked her, "Jennifer, how are you? Where are you? What are you doing now?"

"Well, I'm back in our house, you know. I've come back home. I've been here since Mother died, and I guess I'm doing okay. Oh, Judy, it's really you! I'm so happy . . ."

Happy was the last thing that Jennifer sounded, though; her voice was almost tearful.

"Oh, Jennifer." I was assailed by an overwhelming affection

for my friend, mixed with sadness over whatever ailed her just now, including being so drunk. I had not even known that her mother was dead. Nicola—Nickie Cartwright, whom I had also cared about a lot.

My own parents had both been dead for some time, which is one reason I had had no news from Santa Barbara. Also, since they died of so-called alcohol-related ailments, I was perhaps unreasonably alarmed at Jennifer's condition. A nervous stomach, which is no stomach at all for booze, had kept me, if unwillingly, abstemious.

"And oh!" Jennifer's voice sounded indeed much happier now. "I forgot to say happy birthday. Judy, Jude, happy happy birthday! Every year I think of you today, even if I haven't ever called you."

"You're so good to remember," I told her. "But really, tell me how you are."

"Oh, you tell me! First off, you tell me just what you have on." Such a perfect Jennifer question—or Nickie: Nickie too would have asked me what I was wearing, in order to see me, and to check on how I was.

To please Jennifer, I should have described a beautiful, colorful dress, but a lack of imagination, I believe, has kept me honest; I tend to tell the truth. My former (only) husband observed that I had a very literal mind, and he might have been right, as he was with a few other accurate accusations. In any case, I told Jennifer, "Just a sweater and some pants. My uniform, I guess. But they're both new. Black. Actually, I'm going out to dinner. This man I met—"

Jennifer began to laugh, her old prolonged, slow, appreciative laugh, and I thought, Well, maybe she's not so drunk. Just a little tipsy, maybe, and overexcited.

"Oh, Jude." Jennifer was laughing still. "You're going out

on a date, and we're so old. But you sound like you're about sixteen, and wearing something pink and gauzy."

Rational, sober person that I am, I could have cried.

But Jennifer went on in a conversational, much less drunken way. "I think about you so much," she said. "And everything back then. All the fun we had. Of course, since I've moved back here it's all easier to remember."

"I'm really sorry to hear about Nickie," I told her.

"Well, just one more terrible thing. Everyone gets cancer, it seems like to me. Honestly, Jude, sometimes I think being grown up really sucks, don't you? To use a word I truly hate."

"Well, I guess."

"Your parents die, and your husbands turn out bad. And your kids—oh, don't even talk to me about kids."

Her voice trailed off into a total silence, and I thought, Oh dear, she's fallen asleep at the telephone, out there in California, in that house I know so very well. The house right next door to the house where my parents and I used to live—in fact, its architectural twin—on what was called the Santa Barbara Gold Coast, up above the sea. I wondered what room Jennifer was in—her own room, in bed, I hoped. I called out "Jennifer!" over all that space, Minnesota to California. Calling out over time too, over many years.

Her laugh came on again. "Oh, Jude, you thought I'd gone to sleep. But I hadn't, I was just lying here thinking. In Mother and Dad's big old bed. You remember?"

"Oh, of course I do." And with a rush I remembered the Sunday morning when Jennifer and I had run into the Cartwrights' bedroom, I guess looking for the Sunday papers, and there was blond Scott and blonder Nickie in their tousled nightclothes, lying back among a pale-blue tangle of sheets. Not making love, although I think we must have caught them soon after love. They may have moved apart as we came in; Scott's hand still lingered in Nickie's bright, heavy uncombed hair. At the time, I was mostly struck by their sleepy affection for each other, so clearly present. I can see it now, those particular smiles, all over their pale morning faces.

The room, with its seascape view, was almost identical to my parents' bedroom, and their view. My parents slept in narrow, separate beds. They were silent at home except when they drank, which loosened them up a little, though it never made them anywhere near affectionate with each other.

In any case, I surely remembered the Cartwrights' broad, blue-sheeted carved-mahogany bed.

I asked Jennifer, "Your father—Scott died too?" Although I think I knew that he must have. But I used to see Scott Cartwright as the strongest man I ever knew, as well as the most glamorous, with his golfer's tan, and his stride.

"Just after your mother died. They were all so young, weren't they? Dad had a stroke on the golf course, but maybe that's the best way to go. Poor Mother was sick for years. Oh, Judy, it's all so scary. I hate to think about it."

She had begun to trail off again, and partly to keep her awake, in contact, I asked her if she had married more than once; I thought I had heard her say "husbands," plural, but it was hard to tell, with her vagueness, slurring.

But "Oh, three times!" Jennifer told me. "Each one worse. I never seem to learn." But she sounded cheerful, and next she began to laugh. "You will not believe what their names were," she said. "Tom, Dick, and Harry. That's the truth. Well, not actually the whole truth—I can't lie to my best old favorite friend. The whole truth is, the first two were Tom and Dick, and so when I went and got married the third time I had to call him Harry, even if his name was Jack."

I laughed—I had always laughed a lot with Jennifer—but at the same time I was thinking that people from single, happy marriages are supposed to marry happily themselves. They are not supposed to make lonely, drunken phone calls to old, almost forgotten friends.

Mostly, though, I was extremely pleased—elated, even— to have heard from Jennifer at all, despite the bad signs, the clear evidence that she was not in very good shape. As we hung up a few minutes later, I was aware of smiling to myself, the happy recipient of a happy birthday present. And like most especially welcome, sensitive presents, this gift from Jennifer was something that I had not known I needed, but that now I could no longer do without: a friend for talking to.

I went out for dinner with my new beau in a rare light-hearted mood, but I may have seemed more than a little abstracted. I was thinking of Jennifer, her parents, and California.

When Jennifer and I were friends, all that time ago, I truly loved her, but I also coveted almost everything about her: her golden curls, small plump hands, her famously sunny disposition, but most especially and most secretly I envied her her parents. I wanted them to be mine.

I have since learned (hasn't everyone?) that this is a common fantasy; Freud tells us that many children believe they have somehow ended up with the wrong set of parents. But at the time I naturally did not know this; guiltily I felt that only I had such an evil wish, to be rid of my own parents and moved in with another set. If it could somehow be proved, I thought, that I had been stolen by this dark and somber couple with whom I lived, while all along I was really a Cartwright child—then I would be perfectly happy. And if Jennifer's parents were mine, then of course Jennifer and I would be truly sisters, as so often we spoke of wishing that we were.

From the moment I saw them, even before seeing Jennifer, I was drawn to Scott and Nickie Cartwright, a tanned couple getting out of a new wood-paneled station wagon to look at a house for sale, the house next door to our house. I liked their bright splashy clothes, and the easy, careless way they walked and laughed; I wanted them to be the people to buy that house.

I thought that they looked too young to be parents; that they turned out to have a little girl just my age was a marvelous surprise, a bonus, as it were.

My own parents did not like the look of the Cartwrights, at first. "Lots of flash" was my Vermont mother's succinct summation. And my father's: "That garden they're buying needs plenty of solid work. I hope they know it." But fairly soon the four grown-ups took to dropping in on each other for a cup of coffee or a Coke, maybe, during the day; and at night they all got together for drinks. The Cartwrights, from St. Louis, had a sort of loose-style hospitality to which even my fairly stiff-mannered parents responded.

What must initially have won my stern parents' approval, though, was the Cartwrights' total dedication to their garden. Even before actually moving in, they began to spend their weekends digging among the dahlias, pruning hibiscus, trimming orange blossoms, and probing the roots of ivy. And once they lived there, all during the week beautiful Nickie in her short red shorts could be observed out clipping boxwoods, often mowing the lawn. And watering everything.

On weekends, around dusk if not sooner, the four of them would start in on their Tom Collinses, gin rickeys, or fruity concoctions with rum. Eventually one of the grown-ups (usually Nickie Cartwright) would remember that Jennifer and I should have some supper, and the two men (probably) would go out for some fried clams or pizza. Later on they would pretty much forget all about us, which was fine with Jennifer and me; we could stay up as long as we liked, giggling and whispering.

All the grown-ups that I knew at that time drank; it was what I assumed grown-ups did when they got together. Jennifer and I never discussed this adult habit, and "drunk" is not a word we would have used to describe our parents, ever. "Drunk" meant a sort of clownish, TV-cartoon behavior.

My parents as they drank simply talked too much; they told what seemed to me very long dull stories having to do with Santa Barbara history, early architects, all that. The Cartwrights, being younger, listened politely; Nickie laughed a lot, and they sat very close together.

Certainly my parents were never clownish or even loud; God knows they were not. In a bitter, tight-mouthed way they might argue at breakfast; a few times (this was the worst of all) I could hear my mother crying late at night, all by herself.

Because I had never heard them do so, I believed that the Cartwrights never argued, and I was sure that beautiful happy Nickie Cartwright never cried, and maybe she did not.

In the days that succeeded that first phone call from Jennifer, I thought considerably about her, about her parents, and mine. With terrible vividness I remembered the strength of my yearning for the Cartwrights, and I was assailed—again!—by the sheer intensity of all that childhood emotion, my earliest passions and guilts and despairs.

Quite as vividly, though, I also remembered the simple fun that we used to have, Jennifer and I, as children, especially on

the beach. Since I had always lived there in Santa Barbara, on
the California coast, and the Cartwrights were originally from
inland Missouri, I was Jennifer's guide to the seashore. Bravely
kicking our sneakers into tide pools, Jennifer and I uncovered
marvels: tiny hermit crabs, long swaying seaweed, all purple.
Anemones. Jennifer would squeal at dead fish, in a high,
squeamish way, as I pretended not to mind them.

I also showed Jennifer the more sophisticated pleasures of
State Street, the ice-cream parlors and the hot-dog stands. As
we both grew up a little, I pointed out the stores. Tweeds &
Weeds, my mother's favorite, was always too conservative for
the Cartwright ladies, though. Nickie loved frills and lots of
colors; she dressed herself and Jennifer in every shade of pink
to tangerine. My mother ordered almost all of my clothes from
the Lilliputian Bazaar, at Best & Company.

Undoubtedly the tide pools and my happy fascination with
them to a great extent determined my later choice of a career,
although a desire to displease and/or shock my parents must
have figured largely also. Biology to them connoted sex, which
in a general way they were against.

And possibly in some way of my own I made the same connection. In any case, I am forced to say that so far I have shone
neither professionally nor in a romantic way. I did achieve a
doctorate, and some years later an assistant professorship, at
relatively early ages, but I do not feel that I will ever be truly
distinguished.

As one of my more kindly professors put it, my interest in
marine biology could be called aesthetic rather than scientific.
I excel at drawing—urchins, starfish, snails.

As to my romantic history, it got off to a shaky start, so to speak, with my marriage to a fellow biologist, a man who after two years of me announced that colleagues should not be married to each other. (This could be true, but it had been his idea, originally.) He left me for a kindergarten teacher in Chicago, where his next teaching job happened to be. I became involved with an elderly musicologist, who was married; later with a graduate student in speech and drama, who, I came to believe, used coke, a lot of it.

Three men, then—my husband and two subsequent lovers—who presented certain problems. However, surely I do too? I am hardly "problem-free" or even especially easy to get along with. I am moody, hypersensitive, demanding.

In any case, these days as far as men are concerned I am running scared.

After that first birthday call, Jennifer telephoned again, and again. She seemed to have an unerring instinct for the right time to call, not an easy feat with me. (I once knew a man who always called me when I was brushing my teeth; I used to think that if I really wanted to hear from him I had only to get out my toothbrush.) In Jennifer's case, though, it may have been that I was simply so glad to hear from her.

I gathered that her present life was quite reclusive; she did not seem to know where anyone else whom we had known was now. I gathered too that she was quite "comfortably off," to use an old phrase of my mother's. My mother thought "rich" a vulgar word, and perhaps it is. Anyway, I was very glad that Jennifer was comfortable.

As I got used to talking to Jennifer again, sometimes I would find myself scolding her. You should get out more, take walks, get exercise, I would say. Go swimming—there must be a pool around. And what about vitamins? Do you eat enough? And Jennifer would laugh in her amiable way, and say she was sure I was absolutely right.

Jennifer's memory for long-gone days was extraordinary, though. She reminded me of the day we decided that to be kidnapped would be a thrilling adventure. We put on our best dresses and paraded slowly up and down State Street, conversing in loud voices about how rich (we liked the word) our parents were. Yachts, Spanish castles, trips on the *Queen Mary,* penthouses in New York—we mentioned all the things the movies had informed us rich people had, and did.

"You had on your striped linen," Jennifer perfectly recalled, "and I was wearing my lavender dotted swiss." She laughed her prolonged, slow chuckle. "We just couldn't understand why no one picked us up. Rich and adorable as we were. You remember, Jude?"

Well, I would not have remembered, but Jennifer brought it all back to me, along with our beach walks, the beautiful tide pools, the white sand, the rocks.

I began to look forward to those phone calls. I felt more and more that my connection with Jennifer was something that I had badly missed for years.

I believe I would have enjoyed talking to Jennifer under almost any circumstances, probably, but that particular fall and winter were bad times for me—and seemingly the rest of the world: Ethiopia, Nicaragua. In the American Midwest, where I was, unemployment was rife, and terrible. And to make everything worse the snows came early that year—heavy, paralyzing.

In a personal way, that snowed-in, difficult winter, things were especially bad: I was not getting along at all with my latest beau, the man who came to take me out to dinner on the night of Jennifer's first phone call. This was particularly

depressing since we had got off to a very, very good start—not
fireworks, not some spectacular blaze that I would have known
to distrust, but many quiet tastes in common, including cats
(he had five, an intensely charming fact, I thought, and they
all were beautiful tabbies). The truth was that we were quite
a lot alike, he and I. Not only our tastes but our defects were
quite similar. We were both wary, nervy, shy. Very likely we
both needed more by way of contrasting personality—although his former wife had been a successful actress, flamboy-
ant, a great beauty, and that had not worked out too well,
either. In any case, we further had in common the fact of being
veterans of several mid-life love affairs, both knowing all too
well the litany of the condition of not getting along. We ex-
hibited a lessening of interest in each other in identical ways:
an increase in our courtesy level. We pretended surprise and
pleasure at the sound of each other's voice on the phone; with
excruciating politeness we made excuses not to see each other.
(At times it occurred to me that in some awful way I was
becoming my parents—those super-polite role models.) And
then we stopped talking altogether, my lover and I.

The next year was to be my sabbatical from the college, and
none of my plans seemed to be working out in that direction,
either. Nothing available at Woods Hole, nothing in San
Diego. Or Berkeley, or Stanford.

Around March, with everything still going bad and no signs
of spring, I realized that I had not heard from Jennifer for
several weeks. Some instinct had all along advised me that I
should wait to be called, I should not call Jennifer. Now, however, I did; I dialed the number in Santa Barbara. (Easy
enough to come by: Jennifer, an unlikely feminist, had returned to her maiden name.)

It was not a good conversation. Jennifer was very drunk, although it was only about six at night, California time. She was drunk and sad and apologetic, over everything. She was extremely polite, but I felt that she was not even certain who I was; I could have been almost anyone. Any stranger, even, who happened to call, selling magazine subscriptions or offering chances to buy tax-free municipal bonds.

I was seriously worried, and after a little time I came to certain serious decisions.

I did the following things, in more or less this order:

I made an appointment and went to see the head of my department, and after some conversation, some argument, we struck up a bargain, of sorts. I would be granted a year's leave of absence (this involved less pay than a sabbatical, which was one of my selling points), and in return for this great favor I would teach an extra section of the general-science course for freshmen on my return.

I put up a notice on the bookstore bulletin board about renting out my house; from a great many applicants (probably I should have asked for more money) I selected a nice young couple from the Music Department. The only problem was that two people in the house would need all my small space; I would have to store everything but the furniture.

Through a national real-estate outfit I located a real-estate agent in Santa Barbara, who (this seemed an omen, a sure sign that I was on the right track) had a listing just a couple of houses down from Jennifer's—a garage apartment, mercifully cheap.

I called Jennifer, and as though it were a joke I said that I was coming out for a year, to take care of her.

. . .

And that is where I am now, and what I am doing. My apartment is in an alley half a block from Jennifer's house, the Cartwright house—and of course from my parents' house, too, the house that I sold when they died: my money for graduate school. My apartment is tiny, but since I am not there much, no matter. I have room for my drawing board, shelves of books and stacked papers; and outside there is a tiny scrap of a yard, where a neighbor cat comes to visit occasionally (he is beautiful—a pale-gray, long-eared, most delicate-footed creature).

I am beginning to run into a problem with space for clothes, though. When I first got here, Jennifer was so depressed, she said, by the darkness of my wardrobe ("Judy, you can't go around like that, not out here, in those professor clothes") that we have done a lot of State Street shopping, by way of brightening up my look. "But you're wonderful in that red silk," Jennifer insisted.

Jennifer herself, for a person who drinks or who has drunk that much, looks remarkably well. Needless to say, I was more than a little nervous about seeing her again. How would she look? I was so scared, in fact, that I gave very little thought to how I would look to her, and I think actually I am the one who has aged more. Jennifer is thin, a little frail and shaky on her feet, that is true, but her skin is still good, fine and pink, and her eyes are blue and clear. She just looks like a very, very pretty woman, of a certain age.

The first few weeks of my stay I made all the obvious suggestions having to do with drink: the Betty Ford place, or A.A., or just a plain good doctor. Well, Jennifer refused to go to anything, as I might have known she would—she has always been extremely stubborn. She even says that her doctor says she is perfectly all right. Two explanations for that last occur to me: one, she does not tell her doctor, or did not, how much she really drinks; or, two, the doctor himself is an alcoholic; I've heard that a lot of them are.

I have made a couple of strong advances, though. One is in terms of nutrition. I have instituted a heavy regimen of vitamins, and also I do most of the shopping and cooking. I go down to the docks for fresh fish, and on Saturday mornings there is a Farmers' Market, with lovely California vegetables and fruits. We eat very well, and I am sure that Jennifer eats a lot more with me around.

Another considerable advance is that Jennifer has entirely given up hard liquor, and now only drinks wine, white wine. In her big blue Ford station wagon we drive down to the new liquor store just off State Street. A handsome, bright-brassy, airy space. We walk around among the wooden crates and bins and shelves of bottles. This particular store deals mostly in California wines, and there are always some interesting new labels. New wineries keep turning up all over the state, even in very unlikely places, like San Luis Obispo or San Diego. We laugh at some of the names, which are often a little outlandish: Witches' Wish? And we admire the designs of the labels. We have even come to conclude that there is a definite correlation between beautiful labels and first-rate wines. Vichon, for example, one of our favorites, has an especially pretty picture on its bottle.

One of the best aspects of this whole venture for me is my discovery that after all I really can drink wine, with no ill effects. When I first came out, I would have one glass of wine at dinner, to keep Jennifer company, as it were. Then sometimes two, then sometimes another at home.

And now, in the late afternoons, though still too early to start over to the Cartwrights'—to Jennifer's house—I begin to think how nice a cool dry glass of wine would taste, and then I think, Well, why not? This is, after all, a sort of vacation for me. And so I pour myself one. I take the wine outside. I sit in one of the half-collapsed but still quite comfortable rattan chairs, in my tiny yard with its minute view of the evening sea, the sky, the burning sun. I sip, and in a peaceful way I contemplate my return to Santa Barbara.

I almost never think about my parents, or those old unhappy days spent here with them, growing up. Our family house has been remodeled almost beyond recognition, for which I am grateful. Only very infrequently do I feel its presence as that of a ghost, looming there just next to the Cartwright house.

I do not worry in the way that I used to about my career—that career, teaching at Minnesota. Marine biology. Sometimes I think I could stay right here forever (someone else could take on the freshman sections), and maybe get into something entirely new. I could walk on the beach and make sketches. (I do that already, of course; I mean I could do it in a more programmatic way.) Maybe someday I would be good enough to have a show, and maybe sell some. Or I could give drawing lessons at some local school. I might even, as we say, *meet someone.* Some nice young bearded man, with leftist views and a fondness for cats. A farmer, maybe; he might wander into the market some Saturday morning, with some lovely artichokes.

Jennifer and I have agreed that I should be the one to keep our store of wine, despite my small quarters. The bottles are stacked in silly places—all over my rooms—some under the bed, for example. When I start over to Jennifer's house at dinnertime, I just bring along one bottle; in that way I can keep a check on Jennifer's intake. Which is now down to a couple of glasses a day, I believe.

It is interesting and to me a little spooky to see how entirely unchanged the Cartwright house is. Everything is just the same, but since it all looks, as always, brightly new—the fabrics on the upholstered furniture, for instance, the cushions and draperies—everything must in fact *be* new. Jennifer must have gone out and found duplicates to replace all the worn-out stuff—and with such precision. What trouble she must have gone to, getting everything just right, getting Nickie's look! Including the flourishing garden, now tended by a nice Japanese couple.

All I said was that it looked really great, what a relief it was to see so little changed—which I know must have pleased Jennifer. She would not have wanted the extreme nature of her pursuit to be mentioned.

As I thought in Minneapolis about coming out here, one of my many conscious or semiconscious fears (worries about Jennifer's looks and her general health naturally being foremost) was a nagging, shadowy worry that as Jennifer and I talked it would somehow come out that Nickie and Scott had been less than the happy, fair, affectionate couple I used to see, and to long for. Heaven knows we would talk a lot, endless talk, and without (probably) coming out and saying so (Jennifer is unusually discreet) she might let me know that sometimes they, like my own parents, used to have recriminatory breakfasts, silences, bitterness. Maybe, even, handsome Scott had affairs, and Nickie cried. That would be a more usual, contemporary ending to their story—and in some circles it would "explain" Jennifer.

But from what Jennifer did say, that sad version would seem not to have taken place; according to her, the sadness was of quite another sort. "My mother was so upset when Dad died she just never got over it, never at all" is what Jennifer said. "Never even looked at anyone else, and you know how pretty she always was."

Well, I do remember how pretty Nickie was, and I can accept that version of her life, I guess. In fact, I would rather; it is what I thought I saw.

"I sometimes wonder if I got married so many times to be just the opposite," Jennifer once mused. "Not to depend on any one person in that way."

"Well, maybe" was all I could contribute. But then I added, "And my parents didn't get along, so I only dared try it once?"

"Lord, who knows?" Jennifer laughed.

Often, as we talked, new memories would assail one or the other of us.

"Do you remember the surprise you planned for Scott one time, on his birthday? The *real* surprise?" I asked Jennifer one night.

She seemed not to, and so I told her: "You led him on into the house when he got home from work, and you told him that you'd found what he'd like better than anything in the world. You brought him to the door of the back-hall closet, and when he opened it up there was Nickie, laughing and jumping out to hug and kiss you both."

"Oh *yes!*" cried Jennifer. "I'd forgotten that, and how could I forget? But you see what I mean, Judy, Jude? Who could ever come up with a relationship like that?"

Who indeed? Most surely not I, I reflected.

But mostly Jennifer and I are not so serious. Our dinners are fun. We remember school friends, boys, our teachers; we go over and over the people we knew and the times we had back then, just remembering and laughing. Not deeply, intellectually scrutinizing, as I might have with other friends, at another time.

Jennifer subscribes to all the fashion magazines, and sometimes sitting there at dinner we may just leaf through a couple. Most of the newest styles are quite ugly, if not down-

right ludicrous, we are agreed. But every now and then there
will be something really pretty; we will make a note to check
it out in the downtown stores.

Jennifer has not taken a newspaper for years, and since I
have been out here I have not really read one, either. I find it
a great relief, in fact, not to know just how awful things have
become. How entirely out of control the whole terrifying
world is.

We did at first go over some of the unfortunate events of
both our marriages, and in a discreet way I told her about my
love affairs. I found that, recounting them to Jennifer, I could
make them really funny. She liked the story about the man
who always called when I was brushing my teeth, and she
appreciated my version of my most recent relationship, the
man and I becoming more and more polite as we liked each
other less. She told me a couple of funny stories about her
husbands, though I think their names are what she most likes
to remember.

Jennifer does not talk about her children, except to say that
she has three of them, all moved East. Three girls. Two work
in New York, one lives on a farm in Vermont—no grandchildren that she has mentioned—and since she never seems to
hear from her daughters I would guess that they don't get
along. But I never ask.

By the time we have finished our dinner, our bottle of wine,
we are both rather sleepy. We get up from the table, and together we walk out to the front hall. Jennifer opens the door,
we say good night; we kiss, and I go outside and listen for the
sound of the lock behind me.

I walk the short, safe distance down the road to my apartment.

If the weather is nice, a warm night, I may sit outside for a
while, something I could almost never have done in Minne-

sota. Maybe I will have one more glass of wine. Maybe red, a good zinfandel, for sleep.

Just sitting there, sipping my wine, I think a lot, and one of my conclusions has been that, all things considered, even living alone, I really feel better and better out here, and I think I have never been so happy in my life.

The visitor cat must by now be on to my habits, for sometimes at these moments I will feel the sudden warm brush of his arching back against my leg. I reach to stroke him. He allows this, responding with a loud purr—and then, as suddenly as he appeared, with a quick leap out into the dark he is gone.

FAVORS

July that year is hotter, the air heavier and more sultry than is usual in Northern California, especially up in the Sierras, near Lake Tahoe. Along the Truckee River, which emanates from that lake, mosquitoes flourish in the thick green riverside bushes and grass. Even in the early mornings—most unusual—it is already warm and damp. An absolute stillness, a brooding quiet.

"If this were Maine, there would be a thunderstorm," remarks Maria Tresca, an elderly political activist, just released from jail. By profession she is an architect. A large-boned, heavy woman, with gray-brown hair and huge very dark eyes, she is addressing the much younger couple who are with her on the terrace of her river house. The three of them have just finished a light breakfast in the dining room, inside; they now sit on old canvas deck chairs.

Having spoken, Maria closes her eyes, as though the effort involved in keeping them open were more than she could manage in the breezeless heat, the flat air.

The two young people, the couple, are Danny Michaels, a

small, gray-blond young man, rather lined for someone his age, serious, bookish-looking; and thin, bright-red-haired Phoebe Knowles, Danny's very recent wife.

"That would be wonderful, a storm," says Phoebe, who seems a little short of breath.

And Danny: "We sure could use the rain."

"Actually, I'd be quite terrified," Maria opens her eyes to tell them. "I always used to be, in Maine. We had the most terrific summer storms." She recloses her eyes.

Danny has known Maria for so long (almost all the thirty-odd years of his life) that nearly all questions seem permitted; also they like and trust each other. However, so far his evident sympathetic interest in her recent experience has been balked. About Pleasanton, where the jail was, Maria has only said, not quite convincingly, "It wasn't too bad. It's minimum security, you know. I felt rather like a Watergate conspirator. The clothes they gave me were terribly uncomfortable, though. Just not fitting, and stiff."

Only Maria's posture suggests discouragement, or even age. On the old rattan sofa she slumps down in a tired way among the cushions, her large hands clasped together on the knees of old corduroys.

And goes on about Maine. "The chipmunks there were much bigger than the ones out here," she tells Phoebe and Dan. "Or maybe they only seemed bigger because I was very small. I haven't been back there since I was a child, you know."

Phoebe and Dan are in the odd position of being both Maria's hosts and her guests: it is her house—in fact, very much her house, designed by Maria for her own use. But it was lent to Danny and Phoebe by Ralph Tresca, Maria's son and a great friend of Danny's. This was to be their wedding present, two weeks alone in this extraordinary, very private house. For which they had both arranged, with some trouble, to take off from their jobs. Phoebe and her best friend, Anna, run a small restaurant on Potrero Hill; Danny works in a bookstore, also on Potrero, of which he is part owner.

Danny and Ralph have been friends since kindergarten, and thus Danny has known Maria for all that time. He and Phoebe have known each other for less than four months; theirs was a passionate, somewhat hasty marriage, indeed precipitated by Ralph's offer of the house. Danny called Ralph in Los Angeles, where Ralph is a sometime screenwriter, to say that he had met a girl about whom he was really serious. "I think we might get married." To which Ralph responded, "Well, if you do it this summer you can have the house for two weeks at the end of July. It's rented for most of the rest."

Not the reason, surely, but an impetus. Danny has always loved the beautiful, not entirely practical house, at which he has often been a guest. A wonderfully auspicious beginning to their marriage, Danny believed those weeks would be.

But after the first week of their time at the house had passed, there was suddenly the phone call from Ralph, asking if it would be all right for Maria to come up and stay with them; Maria was about to be released, after fourteen days in jail. Danny had known about Maria's sentencing; he and Phoebe had talked about it, early on—so severe for an antinuclear protest, and for a woman of Maria's age. But they had not been entirely clear as to when Maria started to serve, nor when she was to get out. And it had certainly not occurred to Danny that Maria might want to come from jail to her house on the Truckee River. However: *Of course,* he told Ralph.

Hanging up the phone, which is in the kitchen, and walking across the long living room toward their bedroom, where

he and Phoebe had been taking a semi-nap, Danny considered
how he would put it to Phoebe, this quite unforeseen interruption to their time. Danny knows that he is crazy about
Phoebe, but also acknowledges (to himself) some slight fear;
he suspects that she is perceptibly stronger than he is. Also, it
was he who insisted on marriage and finally talked her into it,
mentioning their ages ("we're not exactly kids") plus the bribe
of the house. But the real truth was that Danny feared losing
her—he had indecisively lost a couple of other really nice
women; now he wanted to settle down. In any case, although
he feels himself loved by Phoebe, feels glad of their marriage,
he worries perhaps unduly about her reactions.

"You see, it was such a great favor that I couldn't not do it"
was one of the things he decided to say to Phoebe, approaching
their room. "All that time in jail, a much longer sentence than
anyone thought she would get. I think her old protest history
worked against her. I know it was supposed to be our house
for these two weeks, Ralph kept saying that. He really felt
bad, asking me to do this," Danny meant to add.

What he did not mean to say to Phoebe, in part because he
did not know quite how to phrase it, was his own sense that
if Maria were to come up to them, Ralph should come too.
Ralph's presence would make a better balance. Also, Ralph's
frenetic nervous energy, his offbeat wit—both qualities that
made Danny smile, just to think about—would have light-
ened the atmosphere, which so far has been more than a little
heavy, what with the weather and Maria's silences, her clearly
sagging spirits.

However, Dan had barely mentioned to Phoebe that Maria
was getting out of jail on July 19 when Phoebe broke in, "Oh,
then she must come right up. Do you think we should leave,
or stay on and sort of take care of her? I could cook a lot, prison
food has to be horrible. Tell Ralph not to worry, it'll be fine."

All of which led Danny to think that he does not know Phoebe well at all.

Phoebe herself has had certain odd new problems on this trip: trouble eating, for one thing; she who generally eats more than her envious friends can believe, scrawny Phoebe of the miraculous metabolism now barely manages a scant first helping of the good cold rice salads, the various special dishes she planned and made for this first leisurely time alone with Dan. And she is sometimes short of breath. Also, despite long happy nights of love, she has trouble sleeping. All these problems clearly have to do with the altitude, six thousand feet, Phoebe knows that perfectly well; still, does it possibly have something to do with being married—married in haste, as the old phrase used to go?

By far her worst problem, though, is sheer discomfort from the heat, so much heavy sun all day. Like many redheads, Phoebe does not do well in very warm weather, the affliction being an inability to perspire. Instead, out in the sun her skin seems to wither and burn, both within and without. Very likely, she thinks, if it cooled off even a little, all her troubles would disappear; she could eat and sleep again, and enjoy being married to Dan.

However, she reminds herself, there would still be the house. Danny talked about it often; he tried to describe Maria's house, and Phoebe gathered that it was beautiful—impressive, even. Still, she was unprepared for what seems to her somewhat stark: such bare structural bones, exposed textures of pine and fir, such very high, vaulted ceilings. Phoebe has never been in a house with so definite a tone, a stamp. In fact, both the house's unfamiliarity and the strength of its character have been more than a little intimidating. (Phoebe is from a small town in New Hampshire of entirely conventional, rather small-scale architecture.)

Even the bookcases have yielded up to Phoebe few clues of a personal nature, containing as they do a large, clearly much used collection of various field guides, to birds, wildflowers, trees, and rocks; some yellowed, thumbed-through Grade-B detective fiction; and a large, highly eclectic shelf of poetry— Rilke, Auden, Yeats, plus a great many small volumes of women poets. Marianne Moore, Elizabeth Bishop, Louise Bogan. Katha Pollitt, Amy Clampitt. Clues, but to Ralph or to Maria? Ralph's father, Maria's husband, died young, Dan has said; he has spoken admiringly of Maria's uncompromising professionalism, her courage—never a shopping center or a sleazy tract. The poetry, then, might belong to them both? There are no inscriptions.

Thus, occupying the house of two very strong, individualistic people, neither of whom she has met, fills Phoebe with some unease, even a sort of loneliness.

The site of the house, though, is so very beautiful—magical, even: that very private stretch of clear brown river, rushing over its smoothly rounded, wonderfully tinted rocks. And the surrounding woods of pine and fir and shimmering gray-green aspens, and the lovely sky, and clouds. The very air smells of summer, and earth, and trees. In such a place, Phoebe thinks, how can she not feel perfectly well, not be absolutely happy?

Indeed (she has admitted this to herself, though not to Dan), she welcomed Maria at least in part as a diversion.

Though since her arrival Maria has seemed neither especially diverting, as Phoebe had hoped, nor heroic—as they both had believed.

.   .   .

"It would be a lot better if Ralph were here too, I know that,"
Dan tells Phoebe, later that morning, as, barefoot, they pick
their way back across the meadow to the house; they have been
swimming in the river—or, rather, wading and ducking down
into the water, which is disappointingly shallow, slow-
moving, not the icy rush that Danny remembers from previous
visits.

Phoebe, though, seems to feel considerably better; she
walks along surefootedly, a little ahead of Dan, and her tone is
reassuring as she says, "It's all right. I think Maria's just really
tired. I'm doing a vitello tonnato for lunch, though. Remember, from the restaurant? Maybe she'll like that. God, I just
wish I could eat!"

Avoiding sharp pinecones and sticks and skirting jagged
rocks requires attention, and so they are quiet for a while as
they walk along. But then, although he is in fact looking
where he is going, Dan's foot hits something terrible and
sharp, and he cries out, "Damn!"

"What's wrong?"

"My foot, I think a stone."

"Oh dear." Phoebe has stopped and turned to ask, "Shall I
look?"

"No, it's okay, nothing," Dan mutters, striding on past her.

But he is thinking, Well, really, how like Ralph to saddle
me with his mother on my honeymoon. And with Maria just
out of jail, for God's sake. So politically correct that I couldn't
possibly object. Damn Ralph, anyway.

Never having met Ralph, who has been in Los Angeles for all
the time that Dan and Phoebe have known each other (the
long, not long four months), Phoebe has no clear view of him,
although Dan talks about him often. What has mostly come

across to Phoebe is the strength of the two men's affection for each other; so rare, in her experience, such open fondness between men. She has even briefly wondered if they could have been lovers, ever, and concluded that they were not. They are simply close, as she and her friend-partner, Anna, are close. Danny would do almost anything for Ralph, including taking in his mother at a not entirely convenient time.

In fact, his strong, evident affections are among the qualities Phoebe values in Dan—and perhaps Ralph is more or less like that? His closeness to his mother has had that effect? Although so far Maria herself has not come across as an especially warm or "giving" person.

Early common ground, discovered by Dan and Phoebe on first meeting, was a firm belief in political protest. They had both taken part in demonstrations against the Nicaraguan embargo, against South African racism; both felt that there was, generally, a mood of protest in their city, San Francisco, that spring. By which they were encouraged.

And they had had serious talks about going to jail. Taking part in demonstrations is not the same as being locked up, they are agreed.

"It's hard to figure out just how much good it does. Jail."

"Especially if you're not famous. Just a person. Ellsberg going to jail is something else."

"Do famous people get lighter sentences?"

"I'd imagine. In fact, I'd bet."

"So hard to figure. Is it better to go to jail, or to stay out and do whatever your work is and send money to your cause?"

Impossible to decide, has been their conclusion.

However, someone probably has to go to jail; they think that too. So why not them?

. . .

Working in the kitchen, making lunch, Phoebe feels better than she has for several days. Good effects of the dip into the river seem to last, a lively sense of water lingers on her skin. Carefully, thinly slicing the firm moist white turkey (she is good at this, a good carver), Phoebe feels more in control of her life than she has in days just past, no longer entirely at the mercy of weather and altitude. She even feels more at peace with the house. Here in the kitchen, its bareness and extreme simplicity seem functional; the oversized butcher-block table with its long rack for knives is a great working space.

She is happily breaking an egg into the blender, reaching for oil, when she hears the sound of slow footsteps approaching the kitchen. It must be Maria, and the distress that Phoebe then experiences is both general and particular: she likes best to cook alone; in fact, she loves the solitary single-mindedness of cooking. Also, none of her conversations with Maria have been very successful, so far.

Hesitantly, distractedly, Maria comes to stand outside the kitchen doorway. Vaguely she says, "I'm sure I can't help you." She is not quite looking at Phoebe but rather out the window, to the river. "But I did wonder—you're finding everything you need?"

"Oh yes, it's a wonderful kitchen." Working there, it has become clear to Phoebe that Maria herself must be a very good cook; this is the working space of a dedicated person. "I feel bad displacing you this way," she says to Maria.

This earns the most direct and also the most humorous look from Maria yet seen. "You're good to say that. But actually I could use a little displacement, probably."

Phoebe ventures, "Do you have trouble letting people help you, the way I do?"

A wide, if fleeting, grin. "Oh, indeed I do. I seem to believe myself quite indispensable, in certain areas."

They smile, acknowledging some kinship.

"Well, I won't keep you." Maria begins to leave; then, from whatever inner depths of thought, she remarks, "I do wish Ralph were here too. It would be nice for you to meet him here."

"It would have been," agrees Phoebe. "But sometime."

Lunch, though, is no better than breakfast, conversationally, and in Phoebe's judgment even the food is not entirely successful.

They are gathered again on the terrace above the river, joined at the too large round table—scattered around it.

However, partly because he knows that Phoebe is genuinely curious, as he is himself, Danny persists in asking about Maria's time in jail. (Also, he is convinced that talking about it will help Maria.) "What does Pleasanton look like?" he asks her. "I can't even imagine it."

"Oh—" At first Maria's vague, unfocused glance goes out to the river, as though for help, but then she seems to make an effort—for her guests. "It's quite country-club-looking," she tells them. "Very clean and bland." In a tantalizing way, she adds, "It's rather like the White House."

"Really? How?" This has been a chorus, from Dan and Phoebe.

Maria sighs, and continues to try. "Well, externally it's so clean, and behind the scenes there's total corruption." Having gone so far, though, she leans back into her chair and closes her eyes.

Dan looks at Phoebe. On her face he sees both blighted curiosity and genuine if momentary helplessness. He sees too her discomfort from the increasing heat. Her skin is so bright, dry, pink. The sultry air has curled her hair so tightly that it looks uncomfortable. At that moment Danny believes that he *feels* all Phoebe's unvoiced, unspoken sensations; her feelings are his. And he further thinks, I am married to Phoebe permanently, for good.

And, looking at his wife, and at Maria, whom he has always known, Danny thinks how incredibly complex women are. How *interesting* they are.

"In Maine the air never felt exactly like this air," Maria tells them, as though Maine had been under discussion—again. "A little like it, fresh and clean, but not exactly. It's interesting. The difference, I mean. Though hard to describe," she trails off.

"I know what you mean, though," comments Phoebe. "In the same way that all the colors are different, but you can't exactly say how."

"Phoebe grew up in New Hampshire," Danny tells Maria, wondering why this fact had not emerged earlier, or did it?

"Oh, did you really." But Maria has returned to her own privacy, her thoughts. New Hampshire could be across the continent from Maine, for all of her.

The heat has gathered and intensified. Phoebe feels that she will burst, her skin rent apart, the way a tomato's skin will split in heat. What she also feels is a kind of rage, though she tries to tell herself that she is simply hot, that she feels so ill-tempered only because of the weather, the temperature. And, knowing herself, certain bad tendencies, she determines that she will not *say* how angry she is, and especially she will not take it out on Danny.

I love Dan. The weather is not his fault—nor, really, is absent Ralph. Gross, inconsiderate, totally selfish Ralph. Some friend, thinks Phoebe.

She and Dan are lying across their bed, ostensibly napping, although the turgid air seems entirely to forbid real sleep. Naked, they still do not touch, although earlier Dan has asked, "Can I douse you with some cold water, or maybe an alcohol rub?"

"No thanks, but really, thanks." (It was at that moment that Phoebe determined not to vent her ire on Dan, who is genuinely kind, well-meaning.)

They have both been whispering, although no one could conceivably hear them, the rooms being so spread apart; Maria's is several rooms away. "Maria simply clutches that prison experience to herself, doesn't she?" now whispers Phoebe. "Not that she much wants to talk about anything else either."

"Except Maine." Danny tries a small laugh. "Lots of Maine."

"And the way she eats," complains Phoebe bitterly. "Just bolting down a few bites and then a dead stop. It's not exactly flattering. Not that I really care, I mean. Did she always eat like that?"

"I sort of can't remember. Maybe not. I didn't notice, really."

"I have to say, though," announces Phoebe, "I really think this is a very selfish move on Ralph's part."

Dan very lightly sighs, just shifting in bed. "I'm afraid I agree. But people change, I think. Maybe he's pure L.A. these days. More selfish than he used to be. He's been seeing some shrink down there for years."

"That whole culture's so selfish. Crass."

"Oh, *right*."

Feeling a little better, Phoebe reaches her fingers just to

graze the top of Danny's hand. They look at each other; they smile.

Dinner that night, which again is out on the terrace, is in many ways a repeat of lunch, except of course for the menu; provident Phoebe has made a nice cold pasta, with garlicky brandied prawns. But Maria again eats very little, and that most rapidly.

And again she talks about Maine. "The soil was so rocky around our house it was hard to grow flowers," she says. "I've never even tried to plant anything out here."

The night is densely dark, pitch black; in an absolute and final way it is still. And heavy; the air seems weighted. Oppressive, stultifying.

"I do wish Ralph could have been here." It is Dan who has said this, not having at all intended to. It simply slipped out, like a sigh, and now he feels tactless. "But it's great that he has so much work down there," he feebly amends.

"I suppose so." Unhelpful Maria puts her fork down and stares out into the black.

Going about the house, as every night he has—checking door locks, turning off lights—for the first time on this visit Danny has a sad sense of spuriousness: this is not his house, he is much more guest than host. And he recalls now that this place has always been somewhat daunting; its proportions make him feel even less tall than in fact he is. And very possibly Phoebe's deepest reactions have been similar? She too has been made uncomfortable by the house, in addition to the appalling heat, her enemy? None of these facts augur poorly for their marriage, though, Danny believes. Once they are back in San

Francisco, in the cool foggy summer weather, in their own newly painted rooms, then they will be fine.

He admits to himself, however, some real disappointment over what he feels as the failure of connection between Maria and Phoebe. When Ralph called about Maria's coming up, just out of jail, along with disappointment at the curtailment of their privacy, Danny experienced a small surge of happy expectation. Maria and Phoebe, despite obvious differences of age, career, could become great friends, a complement to his own friendship with Ralph. And now that this rapport seems entirely unlikely, Danny recognizes the strength of his hope—his conviction, even—that it might have taken place.

Before starting his tour of the house, Dan urged Phoebe to go and take a long cool bath. "Do you a world of good," he told her. And that presumably is where Phoebe is now, in the bathroom down the hall. (The distance between bathrooms and bedrooms in this house seems an almost deliberate inconvenience.)

As Dan gets into bed, he hears nothing, no sound from anywhere. Outside the window the air is motionless, still; the river is soundless, slow. And although he knows that in a few minutes Phoebe will be there with him, Danny experiences a solitude that seems entire, and final.

And then, around midnight, everything breaks. Brilliant flashes of lightning split open the sky, thunder roars—a sound of huge rocks falling down a mountainside. Slits of light, crashing noise.

Entirely awake, and a little scared, Phoebe abruptly remembers Maria this morning as she talked about thunderstorms in Maine. "Actually, I'd be quite terrified, I always used to be" is what Maria said.

To Dan, who is much less fully awake (he seemed to have trouble going to sleep at all), Phoebe whispers, "I'm just going down to see if Maria's all right."

Slipping into her sandals, pulling on her light cotton robe—in the new blessed cool!—Phoebe begins to feel her way down the narrow, pine-smelling hall to Maria's room at the end, the room nearest the river.

Seeing no light beneath the door, she hesitates, but then very gently she knocks, at the same time saying firmly and loudly enough to be heard across the thunder crashes, "It's Phoebe."

For a moment there is no response at all; then some faint sound comes from Maria that Phoebe chooses to interpret as assent.

Entering, she sees Maria upright in bed, sitting erect but pressed back, braced against the headboard. "Oh" is all she says to Phoebe.

Coming over to stand beside her, Phoebe asks, "Should I turn the light on?" and she reaches toward the bedside lamp, on its table.

Maria stops her, crying, "Electricity—don't!"

Recognizing true panic, Phoebe quietly tells her, "I'll just stay here for a minute, if you don't mind."

In the strange half-light between crashes, Maria reaches for her hand. She says, "Thank you," and can just be seen to smile before quickly releasing Phoebe.

Outside, a heavy pounding rain has now begun, but the thunderstorm seems suddenly to be over; there is only the hard drumbeat of rain on the shingled roof, the thud of water on windowpanes.

Phoebe pulls the small bentwood chair from Maria's desk over to the bed, and sits down.

Maria says, "It was good of you to remember."

"I was a little scared," admits Phoebe.

"The thing about prison," Maria takes this up as though prison had just then been under discussion, "is that they do everything to wreck your mind. 'Mind-fuck,' some of the younger women called it." A faint, tight smile. "But they do. Rushing you all the time. Starting you in to do something, and then right away it's over. Even eating, even that horrible food I never got to finish. And they mix up everyone's mail so you think it must be on purpose. And the noise. Radios. And people smoking."

"Jesus" is all Phoebe can manage to say.

Maria is leaning forward now, her eyes luminous, deep, immense. "At my age," she says. "I mean, I often wonder where my mind is going anyway, without all that."

"That's frightful. Terrible."

"Well, it was terrible. I didn't want to admit it to myself. I got just so plain scared. The truth is I'm still scared."

"Well, of course. Anyone is scared of jail. I'm not even sure I could do it."

Maria's gaze in the semi-dark seems to take all of Phoebe in. "I think you would if you had to, or thought you had to," she says.

"I hope so."

"But I'm worried about going back there," Maria tells her. "If for some reason I had to. Again."

At that moment, however, a new sound has begun, just audible through the steady, heavy rain. And lights can be seen to approach the house, very slowly.

Lights from a car, now visible to them both. Unnecessarily, Phoebe announces, "Someone's coming. A small sports car. Whoever—?"

"It must be Ralph," says Maria, smiling. And she exclaims, "Oh, I do think things will be better now. It's even got cool, do you feel it?" But in an anxious way her face still searches Phoebe's. "Do you want to turn on the light?"

Phoebe reaches to touch Maria's hand, very quickly, lightly—before she pushes the switch.

Standing up, then, in the sudden brightness, smiling, as Phoebe moves toward the door she turns back to Maria; she tells her, "I'll get Danny. We'll go make sandwiches—some tea? Poor Ralph, all that driving. We'll celebrate!"

OCRACOKE ISLAND

Tall and too thin, sometimes stooped but now bent bravely forward into the wind, old Duncan Elliott heads southward in Central Park, down a steep and cindery path—his scattered, shamed, and tormented mind still alert to the avoidance of dangerously large steel baby carriages, and of runners (he must not be run down by babies or by runners, he cautions himself). But most of his thoughts are concentrated on the question of comparative evils: of all that has befallen him lately, and particularly today, what is worse—or, rather, which is worst of all? To have been abandoned by one's fourth and one had hoped final wife, or to have made a total fool of oneself discussing that event—even trying, as it were, to explain it away.

Duncan is a distinguished professor, now an emeritus at a large Midwestern university (for all the good that is doing him now); his wife Cath left the month before, in hot September. Disconsolately traveling to New York, in part to cheer himself up, along with some publishing business, Duncan forgot the possibility of chill late October breezes.

Or—he continues his plaintive litany—is the worst thing

of all to have broken off and lost an old, much filled and re-filled tooth, leaving what must be a conspicuously ugly black hole in the forefront of one's mouth? Oh, what matter which is worse! thinks Duncan then. All of these things have happened (the most recent being the tooth, which only came to his attention out here in the cold) and he can stand none of them.

The runners that Duncan encounters along his way are grim-faced, red, and sweaty, and the young mothers pushing those carriages are scruffy, sloppily dressed; and the babies are—well, babies. Where are the handsome, glamorous pairs of lovers that one used to glimpse in New York, in Central Park? Duncan asks this wistful question of himself, and then he answers (insanely!): On Ocracoke Island. For it is to Ocracoke that Cath has run off with her poet, and in his mind Duncan has just seen the two of them, Cath and Brennan O'Donahue (of all corny, false-literary names), Brennan as handsome and fair as Cath herself is—he sees Brennan and Cath and scores of other couples, all young and blond, all healthy and beautiful, and running, running like horses, on a wild and endless beach.

Cath's gesture—if you call running off to an island with a poet a gesture—was made even less bearable for Duncan by the publicity it drew; she had to choose a famous poet, a Pulitzer Prize–winning, brawling media hero of a poet. A small item in *Newsweek* (Newsmakers) described O'Donahue as having run off to Ocracoke Island "like a pirate, a professor's wife his plunder." Very poetic for a newsmagazine, Duncan thought. Perhaps Brennan himself had written the item? In any case, a lot of people seemed to know whose wife was meant.

At times Duncan feels literally murderous: he will go there

to Ocracoke and shoot them both, and then himself. He has found the place on a map, and it looks as though you had to take a ferry from a town called Swan Quarter. *Swan Quarter?* But surely murder would be a more respectable, even a nobler act than a lot of talk, so deeply embarrassing, so sickly humiliating to recall.

Nearing his hotel, and the promise of some comfort, Duncan begins, though, to dread the coming night. He is to dine with Emily, his second wife: his briefest marriage, that to Emily, and perhaps for that reason they have stayed in touch, have remained almost friends. Emily and Cath have even met, Duncan now recalls, on a trip to New York that he and Cath took just before their marriage. Emily is a painter, beginning to be quite successful. She is, as they all have been, considerably younger than Duncan.

(Younger and in one way or another very talented, the first three of them, Duncan reflects. More talented than he? That was surely a problem with Jessica, the first wife, a poet who took a very low view of criticism. Less so with Emily, perhaps because painting is—well, not literary, and they were not together very long. The worst was Janice, herself a professor, a literary critic. Undoubtedly, Janice in her way was responsible for Cath, who is talentless, a born appreciator.)

But unless he exercises the utmost caution, for which he feels himself much too tired, devoid of resources, Duncan fears that he will simply repeat the follies of the day, with Emily, tonight. He will talk again—perhaps even more ridiculously—about Cath; obviously he will do so, since she and Emily have met. Emily by now is probably—is undoubtedly a feminist; she could finish him off entirely.

At the hotel desk Duncan looks longingly toward the cubbyholes of messages. If only there were a pink phone slip from

Emily, canceling, for whatever reason. (Or a slip saying Cath had called?) But there is nothing, and heavily now Duncan walks over to the elevator. He rings, ascends.

This making a fool of himself began for Duncan at breakfast, in the somewhat dingy dining room of his hotel, as he talked (or tried to explain) to Jasper Wilkes, a former student, and began to babble. "In point of fact I actually encouraged her to have an affair—or affairs; one can't say I wasn't generous. Ironically enough, she could be said to be doing just what I told her to do. In a sense."

Jasper repeated "In a sense" with perhaps too much relish. A highly successful advertising executive since abandoning academe, Jasper is a prematurely, quite shiningly bald young man, with clever, hooded eyes.

"After all," Duncan continued, long fingers playing with his croissant's cold buttery remains, "I'm very busy. And besides . . ." He smiled briefly, sadly, implying much.

"Of course." Jasper's eyes closed, but his voice had an agreeing sound.

Gulping at strong lukewarm coffee—he had just sent back for fresh—Duncan had a nervously exhilarated sense that this was not how men talked to each other, or not usually. Or perhaps these days they do? They are "open" with each other, as women have always been? In any case, he hoped that he had not got out of his depth with Jasper. The coffee had made him feel a little drunk.

And at the word "depth" his mind stopped totally, and replayed, *depth, depth.* He had suddenly, involuntarily seen Atlantic waves, brilliant and mountainous, quite possibly fatal. He had imagined Ocracoke Island. Again.

But could Jasper be in a hurry? Off somewhere? Duncan was conscious of wanting to prolong (oh! all day) this relieving, if highly unusual, conversation. "Precisely," he hastened to agree with what he imagined Jasper just had said. "I intended something discreet and, I suppose I also hoped, something minor. A dalliance more or less along my own lines. My old lines, I suppose I should say." He attempted a modest laugh, but the sound was bleak.

"Right," Jasper agreed. "Something to take up a certain amount of her time and energy. Rather like going to a gym."

"Oh, precisely."

The two men exchanged looks in which there was expressed some shock at their complicitous cynicism, but more pure pleasure—or so Duncan for the moment believed.

The coffee arrived, at which Jasper frowned, conclusively proving to Duncan that he was after all in a hurry; he did not even want more coffee.

"The point is," said Jasper, in a summing-up way, "whether or not you want her back. One. And, two, if you do, how to get her."

Unprepared for this précis, Duncan felt quite dizzied.

Nor was he prepared for what came next, which was Jasper's efficient departure: a smooth rise to his feet, and a firm, sincere handshake. Lots of eye contact. Murmurs of friendship. And then Jasper was gone, last glimpsed as a narrow, animated back departing through the door that led out to the lobby.

Quite disconcerted, and alone with his hot, unconsoling coffee, Duncan looked around. This room had got uglier, he thought, trying to recall what he used to like about it. Surely not the pictures, the big bright oils that all looked like copies of famous works, giving the room a spurious look of "taste"? Never the pictures, he concluded, and surely not the inferior coffee, and fake croissants. Dismally he reminded himself that he had always chosen this hotel for reasons of economy, never for charm.

Now everything seemed to disturb him, though: the room

with its awful art, the bad coffee, and particularly his just ended conversation with Jasper Wilkes. And why? Rerunning that conversation, he succeeded in finding nothing truly objectionable. (Unless that crack about going to gyms—would that have been a "put-on"?) Bright Jasper, though. All agreement, stating and restating Duncan's own views in a clear succinct way. But perhaps that very succinctness was the problem? Especially at the end, just before Jasper hurried off to wherever?

Leaning back into the once pneumatic banquette, for reassurance Duncan stroked his hair, now white but still gratifyingly thick and fine. How Jasper must envy his hair! That in itself could explain quite a lot.

Duncan thought then of the old days, when Jasper as a student came petitioning with his poetry. In conference with Jasper, Duncan might sneak a quick look at his large grandfather clock while pretending to allow his gaze to wander. And apprised of the time, he, Duncan, might then too brusquely sum up his view of Jasper's poem, or poems: Jasper had been all too prolific. And as Jasper at last got up reluctantly to leave, the also departing Duncan, a man in early middle age, might well be off to visit some pert-breasted, ambitious literary girl, for something "discreet," and "minor."

As though Jasper had encouraged him—seduced him, even—into all that talk about Cath, Duncan felt a pained resentment. Especially he resented Jasper's just getting up and leaving him like that—all at sea, almost drowned in ungovernable feelings.

But at lunchtime Duncan could be said to have done it again.

"It was really the way she left that I so much minded," he remarked to his lunch companion, Marcus Thistlethwaite, an English critic, a very old friend. They were seated in a corner of a pretty new Upper West Side restaurant, banks of fall flowers in the windows, filtered sunshine. "I would have given a maid more notice," Duncan added, and then reflected that his analogy had been slightly confused: just who did he mean was whose maid, and who gave notice? He hoped that Marcus had not observed this, but naturally no such luck.

"I'm not sure just who was whose maid," said Marcus, with his ratchety, cropped-off laugh. "But I believe I rather catch your drift, as it were." And then, "Is this quite the proper thing to do with lobster claws?"

"Oh yes, you just crack them like nuts," instructed Duncan, who had just wondered why on earth he had ordered something he had never much liked, and that was at best quite difficult to eat. (And that reminded him inevitably of the seacoast.)

Marcus's hair is thin and silvery, like tinsel; draped across his bright impressive skull, it ornaments his head. Duncan has always been somewhat in awe of Marcus, of his erudition and his cool, uncluttered, passionless judgments. And so why on earth did he have to make that silly remark about Cath, and the dismissal of maids? "Say what you like about New York," he then attempted, striving for an even tone despite a certain pressure in his chest, "the autumns here are wonderful. You know, I walked up through the park from my hotel, and the air—so brisk! And the color of the sky, and those flowers."

Marcus just perceptibly inclined his head, acknowledging flowers, and weather. And then he launched into one of the mini-speeches to which he is given. "An interesting fact, and one that I've made note of"—to those who know Marcus, a familiar beginning, very likely boding no good to his audience, be it plural or singular—"and of which you, my dear Duncan, have just furnished further proof, in any case so interesting, is the human tendency in times of distress at some ill-treatment by a fellow human to complain of the method of treatment, the form it took, rather than the actuality. The cruel event itself is not mentioned, even. A man who is fired from his job invariably sounds as though a little more tact would have made it perfectly acceptable. And a fellow whose mistress has taken off—well, I'm sure you quite see what I mean."

"In my own case, I do think even some slight warning might have been in order," Duncan bravely, if weakly, managed to say. "And she was not my mistress—my *wife*. We'd been married for almost three years."

"My dear fellow, naturally I was speaking in a general way, and you know how I tend to run on. Well, I don't think I much care for these lobsters of yours. What's our next course? I seem already to have forgotten."

What an old bore Marcus has become, so opinionated, so—so insensitive, thought Duncan, once they parted and he began his walk. However, irritation soon gave way to the sound of darker voices, which asked if he himself was not almost as old, and as boring. And perhaps Marcus was less insensitive than he, Duncan, was hypersensitive, an open wound.

At which point he made—or, rather, his probing tongue made—the most unwelcome discovery about his missing tooth.

Back at last in his hotel room, that cold and perilous park walk done with, behind him, Duncan picks up the phone and almost instantly he succeeds (the day's first small piece of luck) in reaching his dentist. Who is reassuring. Nothing to worry about, the dentist tells Duncan, happens all the time. He adds that it probably does not look as unsightly as Duncan thinks it does; and gives him an appointment for the following week.

The bathroom mirror informs Duncan that his missing

tooth, his "black hole," is unsightly only when he very broadly grins, which he can surely see no reason for doing at any foreseeable time.

Lying at last across his oversized bed, eyes closed, Duncan attempts to generalize about his situation; particulars are what finally do you in, he has found—and so he will not think about Cath's pretty shoulders, not her odd harsh mountain consonants. He strives instead for abstraction, beginning some mental notes on jealousy in an older person, as opposed to what is experienced by the young.

When one is young, he thinks, the emotion of jealousy is wracking, torturous, but at the same time very arousing (he has to admit), an almost delicious pain. Whereas when one is older, and jealous, there is only deep, irremovable sadness, deprivation, hopelessness.

(So much for notes.)

Cath: just a pallid, slightly gangling, easily blushing, mild-tempered girl from the land of the Great Smoky Mountains, from whence those consonants, those vowels. But a girl with an amazing ear for poetry, and a passion for it. Cath was (she *is,* oh, surely she still is) literally crazy about the verse of Andrew Marvell, Herrick, Donne. Wallace Stevens (Duncan's own particular enthusiasm) and more recently some women whose names he now forgets. And most recently of all, Mr. Brennan O'Donahue.

Though at first she did not even want to go to his reading. "It's too hot to go anywhere," she complained.

"But you're crazy about O'Donahue," Duncan (oh irony!) reminded her, and he added, "He's just back from Nicaragua, remember? Besides, I do think one of us should go." Duncan sniffed to emphasize the bad summer cold from which he was suffering (and he now remembers that self-pitying, self-justifying sniff with such shame, such regret). "I'm sure the Taylors would come by for you," he added, naming a younger, obsequious colleague, with a silly wife.

Cath sighed. "Oh, I'll go by myself. That way I can come home early. And Bipsy Taylor is such a nerd." Another sigh. "If I can work out what to wear in this weather."

It was an especially hot September, everything limp and drooping, or fallen to the ground. Bleached rose petals on yellow lawns, and out in the woods where Duncan liked to walk the silence was thick and heavy, as though even the birds were prostrate, drugged with heat.

Cath chose to wear her barest dress that night, which seemed sensible, if slightly inappropriate for a poetry reading. But Duncan felt that it would not do to object: he was making her go there, was he not? And so she went out alone, barearmed and braless, in her loose black cotton; her sun-bleached hair loosely falling, her small round shoulders lightly tanned.

You look almost beautiful, is what Duncan thought of saying, and fortunately or not forbore; too often he said things to Cath that he later lived to regret. His suggestion—halfjoking, actually—that she could have an affair had aroused real rage. An obscene suggestion, she seemed to take it as; clear evidence of lack of love. Whereas he was not even really serious (God knows he was not). And so as she left that night Duncan only said, "I hope it won't be too dull for you, my love."

"Oh no, don't worry. But you take care of your cold, now. I put the bottle of C pills right next to your bed."

She came home very late, explaining at breakfast that there had been a party at the Taylors', who lived out of town. She had not wanted to wake Duncan with a phone call. She had driven O'Donahue back to the Hilton, where he was staying. The reading was good. He was nice. She thought she would go downtown to do some shopping. Would probably not be back before Duncan's afternoon seminar.

And Duncan returned late that afternoon, after the seminar that included a sherry hour, to find her note. Gone off to Ocracoke Island, with Brennan O'Donahue.

The Village restaurant in which Duncan meets Emily for dinner is a comforting surprise, however; a most unfashionable homey old-bohemian decor, checkered tablecloths and multicolored candles in fat dark green wine bottles, a look dearly familiar to Duncan, who spent feckless youthful years in this neighborhood. Then he was a handsome young man, very easy with women—with a great deal to say about literature, he thought.

Emily, at least at first, seems determinedly nice. "It's wonderfully corny, don't you think?" she says of the restaurant. "But with our luck this look will come back and be madly fashionable. Oh dear, do you suppose it has, and we're the last to know?" And she laughs companionably. "I'm taking you to dinner," she tells him. "We're celebrating a grant I just got."

"You look splendid, my dear, you really do," Duncan tells her gratefully as they are seated; he has never been taken to dinner by a woman before, and he rather enjoys the sensation. This is feminism? And it is true that Emily in early middle age, or wherever she is, has never looked better. A tall woman, she had put on a little weight, in her case very becoming (but can you say that to a woman?). Short curled gray hair, gray eyes, and very white teeth. She looks strong, and immensely healthy. "You look so—so very *fit*," Duncan says to her. "Do you, er, jog, or something?"

Emily laughs again. "Well, I have, but I didn't like it much. Now I just walk a lot."

"Well, I must say, I'm glad to hear that. I find runners such a grim group, they quite scare me," Duncan confesses.

"Oh, me too, they never smile. But, dear Duncan, why are you smiling in that somewhat odd way?"

"I've lost a tooth."

"Well, we all do," Emily tells him. "But you don't have to twist your mouth that way. It's only a gap."

Quite amiably then she talks about her work: painting, teaching, a summer workshop in Provincetown—until Duncan suspects that she is being consciously nice to him, that she is purposefully not mentioning Cath (whom he himself has determined not to talk about).

Well, if that is the case he surely does not mind; nice is perfectly okay with him, Duncan decides, and then he wonders, *Are* women after all really nicer than men are? (He does not voice this question, however, not just then wanting to hear Emily too strongly agree.)

But Emily does at last bring up the subject of Cath, though gently. "I am sorry about Cath," she says. "That must be rough for you."

"Well, yes, it is. But it's nice of you to say so." Which it was.

"I'm sure your literary friends have been enormously comforting, though," Emily in a changed tone goes on, her irony so heavy that Duncan is quite taken aback until he remembers just how much she disliked his "literary" friends, especially Jasper Wilkes, who was still a poet when Emily knew him.

Duncan can only be straightforward with her now. "You're right," he says. "The friends I've talked to have succeeded in making me feel much worse. I had it coming, seems to be the general view."

Emily smiles, her eyes bright. "Oh, you could say that to almost anyone, I think. It's even said to cancer patients. But it really doesn't seem to me that you've been any worse than most men are."

Grasping at even this dubious compliment, Duncan smiles, and then he further complains, "You know, even well-deserved pain is painful."

"Of course it is."

Why did he ever leave Emily, who is as intelligent as she is kind—and attractive? But he did not leave Emily, Duncan then recalls; Emily left him, with sensible remarks about not being cut out for marriage, either of them. Which did not stop her from marrying an Indian painter a few years later, and a sculptor soon after that—nor did it stop Duncan from marrying Janice, and then Cath.

In any case, kind or not, right or wrong, Emily is far better to talk to than Jasper or Marcus. Duncan feels safe with Emily—which leads him to yet another confession. "I did one really dumb thing, though. At some point I told Cath that she should have an affair. Of course I spoke in jest, but can she have taken me seriously?"

Emily frowns. "Well, jesting or not, that's really worse than dumb. That's cruel. It's what men say to wives they want to get rid of."

"Oh, but I surely didn't mean—" Crestfallen Duncan.

Fortunately just at that moment the food arrives, and it is after some silence between them that Emily asks, "You do know that she'll be back?"

"Oh no, no, of course I don't know that at all." Duncan feels dizzy.

"Well, she will. She's basically very sensible, I think. She'll see that Brennan O'Donahue is no one to live with. Running off with poets is just something young women do. Or some of them do."

"Oh? They do?"

"She'll come back, and if you want her to stick around you'd better be very kind. Just remember, a lot of women have been really nice to you. Be understanding. Sensitive. You're good at that."

He is? Entirely flustered, Duncan gulps at wine, hitherto untouched in his swirled dark blue glass. "I find it extremely hard to believe that you're right," he tells Emily, "that she's coming back."

"You just wait." She gives a confident flash of her regular, somewhat large teeth, and then she frowns. "The real problem may be whether or not you really want her back."

"Oh, that's more or less what Jasper said."

Emily's frown becomes a scowl. "*That* expert. Well, probably you shouldn't listen to anyone, really. Just see what happens, and then see what you feel like doing about it. But I'll bet she does come back. And quite soon, I'd imagine."

Once more picking up his key at the hotel desk, as he notes the absence of any phone message, nothing pink, Duncan's tremulous, wavering heart informs him that he has actually feared as much as he has been hoping for a message from Cath. He is so tired, so extraordinarily tired; he has neither the stamina for Cath's return nor for her continued absence. Which is worse? Oh, everything is worse!

In his room, in bed (so depressing, the great size of hotel beds, when you travel alone), feeling weakened rather than tipsy from the moderate amount of wine that he has drunk, nevertheless Duncan's imagination begins to wander quite wildly, and he thinks again of assaulting Ocracoke—oh, the whole bloody island, all those couples, the tall blond lovers, all racing around. As waves crash, as winds hurl sheets of sand, maybe even a hurricane.

Sleepless, disoriented, Duncan feels the sharp anguish of someone very young—of a young man whose beautiful wife has been stolen away. The forsaken merman.

He feels in fact as though he had been forsaken by everyone—by Jasper and by Marcus, even by Emily, with her great superior health and all her hoards of female wisdom. By Cath especially of course, and by Brennan O'Donahue. By all the people on Ocracoke Island—that most beautiful, isolated and imperiled scrap of ground, the one place to which he can never, ever go, and for which Duncan's whole tormented land-locked soul now longs.

ON THE ROAD

BOISE

Some trick of lighting in this particular small, low-ceilinged auditorium makes the audience more visible than most audiences are, here in Boise—but is Boise in Idaho or Utah? The lecturer, a woman named Brendan Hallowell, decides that it must be Idaho; Salt Lake City, Utah, is where she was last night, when, lecturing, she could see no one at all out there. In any case, as she approaches the end of her talk, she can see faces, mostly women's, all quite rapt, and so—so surprised. She is not what they expected; she does not look like her photographs, does not sound like her published work, which is highly serious, slightly academic. But quite startlingly (especially to herself), now, this year she is widely popular, sought after. A success. On a lecture tour.

Coming to the end more quickly than anyone would have imagined—those sympathetic, slightly startled faces seem to expect more, possibly more than she can give them?—Brendan feels her hair begin to fall down from its knot, her hair slipping down to her shoulders, so straight and slippery, such difficult hair. Red hair, quite unexpected from the black-and-white jacket photos, in which Brendan looks tall and composed, not a small, squarely built red-haired woman, now becoming a mess.

Years back, in her graduate student days, Brendan's hair was always a mess, and her small apartment, in Madison, Wisconsin, was messy too, quite hopeless, but intellectually she was never in disarray. At that time she began a series of scholarly studies of "creative women" (even then she herself winced slightly at the term), mostly somewhat offbeat; avoiding Virginia Woolf, she concentrated on Mrs. Gaskell, Emily Hale, Hepzibah Menuhin, and the almost unknown sisters of Jascha Heifetz. She continued in that vein with occasional articles after her doctorate, her various teaching jobs, her marriage; even married to punctilious, hyper-efficient Tom, for whom she made every effort at neatness, efficiency, Brendan continued to write her feminist but not strident, scholarly but not dry articles. And now her new book is a big success: a sort of collected works, a hotshot young editor's compendium of many of those articles, entitled (by the editor) *Sex and Creativity.*

But still her hair falls down, and her new shoes hurt.

"—for the act of creation is, after all, an act of love." Repeating her final sexual metaphor, her essential message, Brendan tries to remember the hotel room to which here in Boise, Idaho, she will eventually go, to which she will mercifully be released. A Hyatt? She thinks not; no, that was in Salt Lake, in Utah, and before that in Winnetka, Illinois, and Albany, New York. Brendan lives with Tom in Bethesda, Maryland, but sometimes she has trouble remembering that house, and even Tom shifts in and out of focus in her mind.

Tom was opposed to this trip, but he never quite said why.

Was he afraid that she would not enjoy it? So far this has certainly been true, as Tom, a lawyer and more experienced in these matters, would have known; still, that seems just slightly unlikely, as does a possible fear on his part that she might "meet" someone, Tom being neither markedly solicitous nor sexually insecure. The point is, she can't quite tell what he meant, or felt. They do not—ever, quite—communicate.

And now, as Brendan wades down into those faces, those bodies, and that applause, with a sudden clarity she does recall her room, here in Boise, so unlike other rooms, in other hotels, how could she have forgotten? It is oddly shaped, very high, with long windows, and Victorian as to decor: a spindle bed, a small, ornately carved bedside chair, white-ruffled vanity table.

"You mean so much—"

"—for years!"

"—enjoyed so much—"

"Good of you—"

Pushing at her hair, and longing for wine (is Boise dry, or is that Utah?), Brendan accepts it all, with her wide impersonator's smile: she is impersonating a successful woman, a woman whom everyone loves, who has something to say to people. Although she wishes, really, that someone would hand her a comb, or some hairpins; all hers seem to have fallen somewhere.

Or a glass of wine.

Or she really wishes that from out of this undistinguished, overeager crowd a dark man would emerge, a large man with a knowing look, a serious smile. They would talk for a while, discreetly, very likely finding friends in common (academic circles are like that, she knows; he could have also been at Wisconsin, have studied there, possibly in some related field).

They would drink some wine together, killing time until in an offhand way he would offer to take her back to her hotel, her funnily named hotel, with its old-fashioned wooden bar in the lobby. The hotel that she now remembers vividly, and longs for.

"Ms. Hallowell, can I get you a glass of wine?"

"Oh yes, thank you. I'd love one, so nice—" Nerves, as always, make Brendan talk too much. How nice it would be, she sometimes thinks, if at the end of a lecture she should conveniently lose her voice.

She watches as the girl goes off for wine.

Many of these women at the present lecture are extremely young, young girls, undergraduates, from the look of them, with pale, intense faces, unkempt hair, and saggy sweaters. And yet how appealing they look! And how enviable, with nothing much expected of them but work, those so easily come-by good grades. How Brendan envies them now, their happy companionableness among themselves, their passionate love affairs with sexually guilty (but sexy, very), intellectual young men.

"Do you mind if I ask, are you, uh, married, Ms. Hallowell?" The girl, who has brought back wine, has hair as red as Brendan's, but hers is curly, very short. She is blushing, asking this bold question.

"Oh yes, I mean, yes, I am married for quite a long time. Seven years, is that long?" Brendan laughs, to her own ears an odd, high sound. "My husband is a lawyer, in Washington." As though that explained anything.

Emboldened, though blushing still, the girl further asks, "Children?"

"Oh no, I mean actually not. I somehow can't imagine, I mean, can you? Children?"

Brendan understands at least two things at that moment:

one, that she is not making sense; and, two, that it does not matter at all what she says at this point. Only her smiling is important, and the fact that she gets out words.

On the girl's pink, freckled face unspoken questions still appear, which Brendan is able to read. What kind of marriage do you have, Ms. Hallowell? Uh, open? What is he like? What is it like to be you?

Their marriage is not open—or not explicitly so, if at all. Like many highly educated, generally talkative people, Brendan and Tom do not talk easily about themselves, not personally, and not to each other—especially not to each other.

Brendan seriously doubts that Tom "sees" anyone else while she is away. High-minded, somewhat austere, Tom is also incredibly, unspeakably busy, always. A familiar successful-people marriage: his energy is drained, consumed in work, while Brendan's is not, or not quite. Conventionally enough, they make love on Saturday nights, and Brendan wistfully imagines Sunday afternoons in bed, long sweaty hours of love. But she imagines them with Tom; her fantasies still cluster around his known ugly-attractive face, his large, gnarled, dark, cumbersome body.

Even her fantasies of unknown men possibly to be encountered on her travels seem under scrutiny to look very much like Tom.

However, in Minneapolis, which is where she will be next week, there is someone whom she might possibly call. Or he could call her; her lectures are fairly widely publicized. He could read in a paper that she is coming, and somehow find out her hotel.

His name is Jack Bishop, and in Madison when they all were undergraduates a friend of Brendan's had a tremendous,

disastrous affair with Jack, at that time a lanky blond basketball star, not at all Brendan's type but extremely attractive,
she thought. In the alumni magazine she has read that he is
now a stockbroker in Minneapolis. She has never met a stockbroker.

Jack, a distinct possibility.

Four days from now until Minneapolis.

ALOFT

Above a vast white tundra of clouds, which are strangely, ee-
rily uneven, heading into brilliant sunshine, going toward
California, the plane could instead be going into outer space,
so smooth and heavy is its passage, so smiling and prepared
for anything are the crew. Or so Brendan imagines.

She is seated on the aisle, on the row just past the dividers
that mark off first class. Thus, no one in front of her, and to
her right two men who she perhaps unreasonably thinks are
gay; in any case, they are quite absorbed in talking to each
other. One of them does not seem well; he coughs a lot, his
hands shake. The other is taking care. They do not in the least
want to talk to Brendan, she feels.

That is quite all right with her, of course it is; generally she
does not like to talk to strangers either. But the total ignoring
of her by these two men is a little bothersome. Do they possibly assume that she is an anti-gay person? Do they automat-
ically dismiss all almost middle-aged women? You are wrong
about me, she would like to say to them. I am nice, I have a
lot of gay friends, sometimes I even think I prefer gay men—
except for sex, of course.

Resolutely looking past them, looking instead out the window and then down at the clouds, Brendan imagines space-

men, astronauts stumbling around on some planet's uneven surface.

She herself is headed not for space, actually, but for Long Beach, California; she will change in San Francisco, but with no time to see the city, just a quick nervous change of planes. A pity: she has never been to San Francisco.

Heading for California, in her mind she is suddenly back in Boise, though, back to the previous night, which she clearly resees—so unhappily! She sees the curly-red-haired girl who walked with her back to her hotel, shaking hands in a formal way, good night, sees herself going into the lobby, with its heavy old oak bar. Alone at last, she then heard a good jazz-piano sound, old-fashioned music, somewhere between Count Basie and Fats Waller. And there in the bar was indeed an elderly black man (actually brown, a huge brown man, with enormous hands) seated at an ebony piano, pounding it out. Smiling to herself and thinking, Great, I could use another glass of wine, Brendan approached the fairly crowded bar. She was almost there, wording her order, white wine over ice, when literally at her elbow there appeared a large dark man. Not the one from her fantasies; this actual man was much handsomer, with fine dark eyes and interesting, jutting eyebrows. And he was saying, "Buy you a drink?"

And Brendan shrugged him off! Dear God, not even politely. Very coldly she said, "No, thank you, I don't drink." (A clear lie: why else would she be heading so eagerly for the bar? Perrier drinkers wear quite different expressions, she is sure.) She then turned and headed for the elevator, hurrying like a schoolgirl, or some classically frustrated, quite deranged spinster lady.

And she lay there in her pretty bed, in her pretty room. All alone.

So dumb. Among other things, her automatic "intellectual" prejudice against handsome men is dumb. It is surely not his fault, that set of regular, harmonious features, any more than the opposite condition would be. He might even have been quite nice, and bright. And in any case their contact could well have been limited to one glass of wine. A half hour, twenty minutes. How silly she was, how wasteful!

And suddenly now, on the smoothly zooming plane, in the brilliant sunshine, seated next to the two men who don't want to talk to her, Brendan feels an almost intolerable wave of isolation. In a loud voice that seems not her own she asks the man next to her, "Do you live in San Francisco?"

He stares for a moment. He is large, with a strong, hawkish nose, and thinning pale brown hair. His skin is unhealthy, too pale. In a hesitant way he says "Yes," and then—dutifully, incuriously—"Do you?"

"No, actually I live in Washington, D.C., and unfortunately I'm not even going to San Francisco but to Long Beach, of all places. Just changing planes, but I hope that some-day—"

Bored with what she herself is saying, Brendan breaks off; she and the sick man stare at each other for a moment before he turns back to his friend, and Brendan desolately opens the paperback on her lap.

LONG BEACH

Very likely by mistake, Brendan has been given a suite in the hotel: two big rooms, an entrance hall, and a vast bathroom. An error: she is hardly big-time on the lecture circuit, not Gloria Steinem, God knows not Kissinger. Feeling that she intrudes—or impersonates!—she walks about the elegantly underfurnished space; she opens drawers, examines a sheaf of notepapers on the desk, reads the lists of food and wine available from room service. She does not read the fire instructions: too frightening.

She rereads the room service menus, wondering what to have for breakfast.

It is four in the afternoon, California time, thus seven in Washington, D.C. Too early to call Tom; probably he would not be at home, and then after her lecture it will be too late. (Last night as she lay so alone in Boise, it was clearly too late for phone calls; Tom would have thought she was drunk—or worse, he would not have been home.)

On the other hand, Tom just might be there now, maybe on his way out to dinner somewhere, maybe Georgetown with some friends?

There are three phones in all, counting the one on the bathroom wall. It is hard to choose for a moment; then Brendan sits down on one of the stiff, chaste beds, and she dials.

For no reason, as she listens to the ringing phone she is breathless. She imagines her empty house, in Bethesda, until after what seemed many rings there is a click, and Tom's voice: a warm, familiar, welcoming *hello.* As though he had expected her to call.

"How did you know it was me?" she first asks (but should she have asked that?).

"I, uh, well, of course it was you. Who else?" Does he sound defensive, accused? She is not sure, but she thinks so.

Brightly she tells him, "You should be here. I have this suite, it's enormous, there must be some mistake."

He laughs, his usual choppy laugh—but is he less friendly, now that he knows who she is? "You're nuts, you really are," he tells her (not for the first time).

Brendan manages a laugh of her own. "Well, I suppose. But it is sort of much, this suite. And I do wish you were here." Dear heaven, surely she is not going to cry?

"Well, it won't be long now. You come home Sunday?"

"No, Saturday. But before that Austin, and Minneapolis."

A small pause before he asks, "It's going well?"

"Oh, I guess." And, meaninglessly, "You know."

The truth is that her lectures, that intense couple of hours on stage before all those people and lights, that time is much less real to Brendan than all the hours alone are, and God knows there are fewer hours of lecturing. Afterwards she is mostly tired, in an extreme, nerved-up way. She cannot, from here, imagine her normal life of work, and productive solitude. Her dinners and bed with Tom.

"Well, actually I'm meeting some people for dinner. In Georgetown. Clients," Tom now says, adding unnecessarily, "It's later here."

"Oh, I know! I just thought I might get you. And actually I'm meeting someone too. God, I just remembered!" Brendan has a dinner date with an old school friend and had almost forgotten; she had forgotten what city she was to meet Lois in (so unlike her—alarming, really). "Lois, you remember her from Madison?"

"Oh Lois, of course." Is he being ironic? Does he in fact have no idea who Lois is, or did he once have an affair with Lois? Or possibly both: he went to bed with Lois and forgot all about it?

"Sweetie," Tom now says, "I'm sorry, but I do have to go. So, I'll see you Sunday."

"Saturday."

"Oh, right. Well, see you then."

"See you."

.   .   .

Lois is blond and thin and tanned and—closely inspected as they exchange the ritual kiss—a little wrinkled; but she is a welcome distraction from that less than satisfactory conversation with Tom (who was he expecting to call? Why can't he remember what day she is coming home?).

In any case, Lois is extremely fit, and initially more interested in Brendan's suite than in Brendan. And this is just as well, Brendan thinks; she has been made aware by Lois's smart, well-fitted pants that she herself has gained more than a couple of pounds on this trip, a predictable hazard of travel, self-improvement articles to the contrary notwithstanding.

"Well, they really did well by you! I'm so pleased. I personally think Long Beach is really great." Lois beams.

"Yes, a suite to myself. I think they must have confused me with someone else, or something. I mean, no one ever—"

"So interesting that you should say that." Frowning in a serious way, Lois perches on the edge of a chair, clasping tidy knees. "I was just reading an article about successful people, so-called high achievers, and it said a lot of them feel like impostors. Someone else has done their work, they think." Lois smiles understandingly, forgivingly.

"But I'm not—"

"But you are! You see? You're living proof." Lois laughs again, very happily.

Feeling scolded, Brendan manages a good-sport smile.

And, having been once struck, that note between them continues through their hurried meal together in the hotel's coffee shop—the dining room is closed for repairs, no time to go anywhere else, which again seems somehow Brendan's fault, along with being famous and overweight (Lois the scold has even mentioned the extra pounds).

Lois, recently divorced, is having the most wonderful time of her whole, entire life, she confides over dinner: her salad, Brendan's grilled cheese sandwich. At some point (rather late, it retrospectively occurs to Brendan) Lois asks, "You're still married to Tom?"

"Yes, still married."

Another point for Lois, who is out there discovering or being discovered by a whole new wonderful breed of men.

And as they part, Lois off to her "date," Brendan to her lecture, Brendan concedes that Lois won their entire encounter. However, it is also true that Lois was trying, competing very hard, whereas Brendan was not, not trying or competing, really, at all. And what was it all about? Brendan wonders. Aren't women supposed to be nicer to each other these days? To be less rather than more competitive? In a discouraged way she decides that in some instances, at least, the grounds for competition have simply shifted, if ever so slightly.

WHY AM I DOING ALL THIS?

This sentence sounds and resounds in Brendan's sleepless mind as she lies in state in her oversized empty suite. Next to her bedroom there is a large terrace of some sort, seemingly roofed in tin. A heavy rain that started up some time ago now thuds arhythmically, loud on the tin. Why am I doing this? Brendan furiously, silently demands of herself.

This tour has nothing to do with my work, she thinks. I am like a traveling salesperson. I am a traveling salesperson, the product being myself.

And with the dreadful, authoritative, false clarity of all insomniac hours, she further thinks, What looked from a distance like freedom and success has become another version of acquiescence. I didn't have to agree to a lecture tour. It is not fun, and I am not learning anything of much use—only not to do it again.

AUSTIN

At breakfast, in Brendan's hotel in Austin, Texas, the air in the dining room is heavy with cigar smoke, thick and stale and inescapable. She is the only woman eating alone in the room, she notes, also noting that the men present are not in the least interested in her as a woman. They all are absorbed in their own jovial conversations, sucking on their cigars or cigarettes. The other women, in their groups, seem almost as alien as the men do: women in business suits and ruffled or bowed silk blouses, with sleek tidy hair. Women as business-like as the men are. Impossible to deduce any personal data about them from their looks. Are they married? Do they have lovers? Do they travel much—enjoy traveling?

As a novelty, or perhaps from some dutiful when-in-Rome feeling, Brendan has ordered grits and "homemade" sausages for breakfast; looking down at them now, she wonders why. The cigar smoke has taken her appetite. Well, good, she thinks as she lays her fork aside. In Minneapolis I'll be a little thinner.

In Minneapolis she will pin her hair securely in a knot, or perhaps she will wear it long and sexily loose, all washed and brushed. In any case, the day after tomorrow, in Minneapolis, she will look adult and genuinely successful, and sexy and available, she has decided. If she is a traveling salesperson she might as well act like one, is one thing that she thinks.

In fact, she will call Jack Bishop from here, from Austin, Texas, and ask him out to dinner, or lunch, maybe Saturday for lunch? And if they end up languorously in bed (her old fantasies of afternoons at last enacted) and if she misses her 4:30 plane—well, so what? Tom seems to believe that she is arriving on Sunday anyway; it might as well be true.

She really does not feel well, though. Something beyond this cigar smoke is making her not well—not precisely sick, but not herself.

She needs a walk; if she does not get some air and a little exercise, she will be in serious trouble, worse than now. *I will be in serious trouble,* she thinks. And this portentous, rather silly-sounding sentence repeats itself to Brendan: I will be in serious trouble, serious trouble, I will be.

Some blocks up the street from her hotel she can see a large pink building, upraised from its surrounding grounds, highly domed, visibly old. Brendan, having left the hotel, now walks in that direction, as many other people are walking, in the delicate, springlike air.

Traveling, she has even become confused as to seasons; it is actually March, she knows that perfectly well, but Boise was so cold; in Boise it seemed the tag end of winter, whereas here in Texas spring warmth. This is one more deeply upsetting fact, she decides; sheer physical displacement is one of the things that is doing her in, too much quick change in both geography and weather. How do real circuit lecturers manage? she wonders. Not to mention the traveling salespeople, with whom she feels, depressingly, a greater kinship.

Just before the capitol building, and surely that is what it must be, with its pillars and cornices, its walks and plaques everywhere, there is a large statue of a soldier in ancient uni- form: the carved white stone announces a monument to the Confederate dead. And Brendan stoops to read the green bronze inscription. It is mostly numbers, an enumeration of those dead, so many Northern (Union) soldiers, so many Confederates. The vastly outnumbered Southerners "fought to exhaustion," says the plaque. And Brendan, who has no "Southern blood" that she is aware of, who shares the views of most liberal intellectuals about many aspects of the South, at that phrase, "fought to exhaustion," Brendan bursts into tears, there in Texas, beside a just budding clump of shrubbery, within sight of the pink granite building.

She is in serious trouble, probably.

MINNEAPOLIS

In the new Radisson Hotel, the lobby bar, where Brendan and Jack Bishop now sit, at a very small table—the bar is Art Deco, sort of. An odd carpet, dizzyingly geometric, black and white, all upraised and separated from the central hall by a series of railings. There is a big grand piano at which last night a large brown man was playing some nice jazz standards as Brendan came in from her lecture. So much like the man in Boise, at that bar. Is he possibly the same person? Is he, like herself, engaged in some crazy tour, traversing miles of states, constantly changing cities and hotels?

In any case, no one there now. A silent piano.

And Brendan and Jack, who have been talking in a fairly animated way, exchanging life stories, now have fallen silent.

Jack is no longer (of course not) the lanky, lithe blond person whom Brendan remembered, and on whom she has been so focused in recent days (it had even begun to seem to her that Jack was the point of all this travel). This present Jack, though, just sipping his second vodka on the rocks, is a trim and very sleek, clearly successful man, of almost middle age. The blond hair is gray and a little thin, but still Jack looks good.

He is divorced, after a couple of marriages about which he

has not said very much; he is probably quite used to lunches with women who have sexy plans for the rest of the afternoon. The only trouble is that Brendan doesn't really like him very much.

All the differences that might be predicted between herself and a Midwestern businessman seem in their case multiplied. They have instinctively avoided any even vaguely political discussion, but Brendan's intuition informs her that he is somewhere to the right of mainstream Republicanism. He goes to Scotland to fish and play golf, his two sons are in a military school (tactlessly Brendan has commented, "Really? I didn't know they still had them"). His tie and his handkerchief, both maroon, are perfectly matched, and his suit is pinstriped, its pants and sleeves perfectly creased.

In no way is he Brendan's type, assuming that she has one; however, he has an available look, and there he is. If she were braver, she thinks, if she were truly liberated, at this very moment she would say, Well, how about some lunch from room service, in my room?

Jack, however, has just summoned the cocktail waitress, whom he seems to know. (Is this possible? Of course it is, this is no doubt a popular bar, as he is no doubt a popular man.) Anyway, he knows her name, Cindy. "Cindy, how's the girl? Well, you can bring us a couple of these good drinks." He and Cindy both laugh, as though he has said something funny, or as though they were such great pals that anything is funny.

Cindy has long straight blond hair, a black miniskirt and frilly white apron, her uniform. Viewed from the back, her black stocking seams are wondrously straight, on her long, impeccable legs.

"Well," says Jack, in a tone that is suddenly warm and expansive, "I can't think of a nicer way to spend a Saturday, can you?"

"Oh no," Brendan murmurs as she thinks, Well, actually I can, quite easily.

Her hair too is long and straight today, all down around her shoulders, and very clean and brushed, if not blow-dried. But maybe too long? And is she too old for such hair? Jack is probably used to much younger women. Like Cindy.

Cindy is back with their drinks, Jack's vodka, Brendan's spritzer (non-drunkenness has been part of her calculation). As Cindy puts the glasses firmly on the table, Jack seizes one of her hands. Is he pressing money into her palm? No, apparently not, as they both laugh—again.

"She's a great girl," Jack remarks, clearly meaning the just departed Cindy.

Brendan murmurs assent, there not being much room for argument, and then Jack repeats what he also said, in just the same words, an hour or so ago: he is sorry he missed Brendan's lecture the night before.

And Brendan says again (with perhaps more emphasis?) that it really does not, did not matter.

But a few minutes later, as Brendan stares across the table at Jack, who is happily settled into his new drink, she is visited by several revelations; they are strangely confused as to order, but at the same time peculiarly clear.

One is that even had she wanted to, it is now too late to say anything about a room service lunch in her room.

And, two, even if she had made such a suggestion Jack might very well in some way turn her down. (And this last is a horrifying thought, but why? Men get turned down by women fairly often; they seem to live with it. Maybe this is something that free women should get used to?) In any case, if Jack had wanted to go to bed with her he could have let this be known by now; it looks as though he would rather drink. Quite possibly he doesn't like her any more than she likes him?

However, the strongest revelation experienced by Brendan just then is the fact that this is the last day of her tour! It is over, and she never has to do this again, not ever, if she does not choose to. This truth is so striking as to clear her head; she feels suddenly braver and stronger. In control.

Her plane, the one she had planned to miss in the course of her fantasied voluptuous afternoon with Jack, the fantasied savior of her trip—her plane to Washington leaves at 4:30. With a little diligence she can just make it, still.

Contriving a sudden look at her watch, with all the emphasis she can muster Brendan exclaims, "Oh dear! I had no idea—so late!" She is aware of not sounding like herself, even of sounding like some silly sitcom woman, but no matter. Jack does not know who she is, and very likely she is presenting him with a person with whom he can deal quite easily; whereas with her, with Brendan as her own true self, everything is hopeless. "My plane," she murmurs. "Tom will be really upset if I'm not on it."

Her instincts about Jack were quite right, seemingly; he is suddenly galvanized, all action. "Well, of course you have to make the plane," he tells her. (Is he anxious to get rid of her? Well, if he is, so what?) "I tell you what, I'll drive you out," he surprisingly says, leading Brendan to wonder at least momentarily if he is not such a bad person after all? Has she been unfair? "Cabs in this town are really chancy," he says.

"But your lunch—"

"Listen, it won't hurt me to miss a meal. I'll just gulp some coffee while you collect your stuff."

And so, about twenty minutes later, Jack and Brendan are headed out on various highways, in Jack's large green Cadillac, toward the airport. He drives very well, Brendan notes; thank God. He does not seem even slightly drunk.

At the security check, to which he has insisted on carrying

her bag, and where they are to part, Jack kisses her passionately, as though they had had an intense romantic interlude.

As though she were someone else.

ALOFT

On the plane, Brendan alternately dozes and drifts into her
own odd, random thoughts. At some point it occurs to her
that this is rather the way she works, allowing herself an almost mindless drift, then trying to pull it into some sort
of focus.

She tries this now, and she realizes that she is still (so irra-
tionally!) embarrassed by that encounter with Jack Bishop. As
though he had read her mind and been aware of her true intentions, she feels turned down, found wanting, sexually. She repeats to herself that she should not mind, if she aims to
function as a liberated woman. And, on the other hand, she
tells herself that very possibly Jack took her at her word; he
thought she just meant lunch—or drinks. Most usefully of all
she repeats to herself that it does not matter; it simply does
not, not at all. And then she sleeps.

Waking somewhat later, looking down far below to the
fenced-off, trapezoidal shapes of farms, from her isolated window seat, she begins to think of those eager young women,
her several audiences. She resees their warm, unsuspicious
faces, feels again their incredible gratitude. And she feels
grateful to them; at this moment she understands that those
fragmentary, often confused after-lecture conversations were
the best part of her trip, its most human exchanges.

She next thinks: I can't wait to be working again.

HOME

She and Tom never meet each other at Dulles; still, as always, Brendan scans the crowds who are there to meet people. Of course Tom is not among them, nice as that would be. Extravagantly, Brendan gets into a cab, and heads for Bethesda.

Arriving at her darkened house, she sees only the porch light left on. And, entering, she sees that the too large house is empty, yielding up no clue as to Tom's whereabouts. It is perfectly clean and neat. Is that Tom's way of welcoming her home, or is he covering tracks? There are no coffee cups in the sink, nor glasses, and the sheets on their bed are fresh.

If he were gone for good, there would be a note, obviously; Tom is neither impulsive nor grossly inconsiderate. However, it is possible that he has managed to forget—again!—that she is to come home Saturday, not Sunday. He is often distracted, his mind somewhere else, presumably on his work.

At least there is a nice new bottle of white wine in the refrigerator: to celebrate Brendan's homecoming? To drink with someone else, his Saturday night companion? Given Tom, this is unlikely; still, it is something that Brendan thinks of as rather defiantly she uncorks the wine and pours out a glass for herself.

In another era, Brendan thinks, or if she were another woman, she could be about to say to Tom, when she sees him, Oh, honey, you were right. I shouldn't have gone. Most of it was lousy, and I missed you. Which, as something to say, has a lot in its favor—including the truth (although "honey" is not a word she ever uses).

However, being herself, and the climate among intelligent women being what it is, Brendan's mood is more adversary.

Why weren't you here? she would (will) be more apt to say. And she will ask him (probably), Why couldn't you remember Saturday, not Sunday?

But as some moments later she recognizes the sound of Tom's car, hears the slamming door, and then not long after hears his footsteps as they cross the creaky porch—lagging steps, but his, unmistakably (and he is alone)—Brendan's mood shifts from defiance and accusation to one in which relief predominates, relief and a certain confusion. She might say— oh, anything at all. She might even say, Why don't we take this nice bottle of wine right up to bed, right now? (After all, it is Saturday night.)

A SIXTIES ROMANCE

She's not up to my usual standards. That was the first thought of Roger Michaels, an architect, on meeting a woman named Julia Bailey, a mathematician. Julia was at last to break his heart, or nearly, but on that April afternoon in San Francisco, back in the early sixties, Roger went on to think, She's not even as good-looking as my former wife. And that dress is a mistake. But she's got good eyes, and she does look intelligent. Probably too intelligent. Well, what the hell. It's only one evening.

Accustomed to being attractive to women, most found him *very* attractive, Roger gave almost no thought to Julia's possible reactions to himself. ("I thought you were sort of overdressed, in that new blazer," she later told him. "And I usually don't like curly hair.") Although he rated himself fairly low on a handsomeness scale (not tall, too dark), there had to be something. Sexiness, he liked to think it was. Or, to put it more elegantly, style. He had a lot of style, he knew that.

This first meeting took place in the narrow front hall of Julia's Twin Peaks flat. Roger was to take her to a party, an arrangement engineered by mutual friends: "Why don't you spend time with an intelligent woman for a change? Try it, you might like it." They suggested that Roger bring Julia to their annual anniversary party, over in Belvedere.

"But a mathematician? Jesus."

However, Roger called her anyway, out of curiosity, he later thought. They fixed on a time, she gave concise directions to her house (a very nice voice, he noted). Twin Peaks was not an area in which he normally spent much time.

And there she was, opening the door to him, with her shy half smile, her pale scarred face (scars from a troubled adolescence, probably), and her rather unusual, yellow-brown, really amber eyes. In her off-pink, not right dress.

They shook hands; he found her hand harder and stronger than he would have expected. It turned out later that she refinished furniture as a sort of hobby (not awfully well, in Roger's judgment), a diversion from the math, which at that time she was teaching at Stanford. She was then an instructor, very hard-worked and underpaid.

In his car they had the requisite conversation about their hosts-to-be. It was established that Julia had known Barbara at college, Sarah Lawrence, and Roger knew Bruce in a business way, through real estate. Roger had in fact designed the house in Belvedere, the site of the party. Roger and Julia could well have met before at one of these annual bashes; they were never to establish whether this was or was not the case—the truth being that if they had met they would not have paid much attention.

"Actually, I don't like these parties very much," Julia confided. "I just seem to go when I can't think of a good way out."

"Well, me neither. But we don't have to stay very long." He could happily take her home early, Roger thought. An early evening, a nice healthy change for him.

. . .

The talk about Bruce and Barbara had only got them as far as the Golden Gate Bridge; thus, to fill in, Roger told Julia something about his recent divorce. "It's a little upsetting, after more than twenty years," he said. "Losing everything you were used to. Especially the kids. But of course I'll get to see them a lot. Take them skiing, stuff like that. Which is not like having breakfast with them every day, though. On the other hand, I do feel a certain optimism about my life. The sixties just getting under way as I start out in my forties. I mean, I think it's going to be an interesting time all around."

"Oh, I really do," agreed Julia. "Except for the horrible war I really like the sixties, so far. The kids I'm getting down at Stanford, even *Stanford,* are really interesting. So rebellious. Not at all like fifties kids."

"Rebellious is good?"

"Sure it is. If it's L.B.J. and the Pentagon you're rebelling against."

"Oh, *right.*"

Roger's glance at her just then took in a shy, semi-defiant look. Insecure, Roger thought. She probably grew up not very popular, smart but sort of out of it. "My former wife would never agree with you," he told her, feeling friendly. "She really gives the kids a hard time about their hair, all that. Still wants to buy all their clothes at Brooks and I. Magnin."

By now they had crossed the bridge and traveled north up the highway. They turned off at Tiburon, and then were almost at Belvedere. And so, as Roger saw it, there was no point now in amplifying the circumstances of his divorce: the affair with Candida (beautiful Candida, where was she at that moment? Candida lived in Marin, and a sudden rush of longing seized Roger, thinking of her). His wife's finding out. Her rage. No point going into any of that with this woman, who was indeed intelligent, a good listener.

Julia was nice, that was clear to him. Too bad about those scars. And the dress.

The party, like all those Barbara-Bruce anniversary parties, was a huge, jammed crush. At some point, maybe after an hour or so, Roger looked across the room and found Julia in a corner, in animated conversation with some group, people she seemed to know. And at that distance she looked considerably better. It was partly her animation; she was clearly enjoying that talk. Also, since she was standing, he could see that she had a very good body. A little voluptuous for Roger's taste, both his wife and Candida were long and lean, tennis players, but Julia was very shapely. He wondered briefly what they were talking about, she and her group, and then he managed to forget her entirely.

Those were days of fairly odd forms of dress among middle-aged, "establishment" people. Both miniskirts and Nehru jackets were in vogue, along with some imitation hippie outfits. In that particular room, at that party, all looks were represented: Barbara, the hostess, wore a white wool minidress with a huge exposed zipper down the front; her husband, bald Bruce, wore a dark blue Nehru jacket and sported a full untrimmed beard. (Roger, whose hair was still very thick and dark, thought Bruce looked a little silly. Talk about overcompensating.) More daring guests were in fringed leather, floppy bedspread-type floral prints. Julia's pink dress was more hippie than mini, a sort of compromise (in Roger's view) supposed to be safe but actually not quite working out.

But the room itself was very good. Roger was always pleased to see it again, to see how his work had held up. He felt that he had made just enough but not too much of the spectacular view, the green lawn that dropped down abruptly in a sheer, rocky cliff to the brilliant bay. And out across the choppy water, beyond Alcatraz and Angel Island, lay San Francisco itself, the bleached-out, pastel city, a Mediterranean back-drop. No, none of that splendor forced itself into the room; it was simply there, as the very large, heavy-boned room was there, a space so elegantly impressive that it took people all unawares, or so Roger had often been told.

An hour or so later, coming upon Julia in a passageway, he said to her, "*Well.*" And then, "I've been looking for you all over," he lied. "About ready to go?"

"Oh sure. Any time."

She was almost too agreeable, Roger felt, as though she had no views or feelings of her own, which he sensed was not so. But a yielding woman, he decided. All give. He himself pre-ferred a little more abrasion. Candida was a pretty feisty num-ber, at least half the time, fussy about small things like just which motel for the afternoon. And he sighed again for beau-tiful Candida, who had said quite clearly that she didn't want to see him anymore. "It's getting too heavy," she told him. "And I don't want any part of anyone's divorce." All that was said through tears, lots of tears, but he knew that she meant it. No divorce, that was one of the rules.

As Roger and Julia crossed the bridge on their way back to the city, an exceptional sunset was in progress out across the bay, beyond the Farallones. Intense, wild, brilliant colors, now just

on the verge of fading. Roger saw that Julia was looking out
that way, toward the sunset, and he gave her points for saying
nothing about it, simply turning back to him with a small
smile.

And then she said, "Those parties. Really, such a waste. I
always wonder why I go. But at least the house is so great.
I always love just seeing it."

Grinning, Roger told her, "That's very nice for me to hear."

"Oh? Oh, of *course,* Barb told me you were the architect. I
really like it," she emphasized. "It's an amazing combination,
elegant and splendid and at the same time extremely subtle, if
you see what I mean. I probably didn't say it very well."

"Extremely well, as a matter of fact. It's about the best
thing I've ever heard."

"Oh. Well." Shyly she ducked her head down.

"But you did seem to like some of the party," Roger said a
little later—still a long way from Twin Peaks (of all eccentric
places to live). "You found some people you knew?"

Julia's laugh had a quick, nervous sound. "People to argue
with, mostly. I seem to be getting a reputation as a real pothead."

"Pothead?" It was not a word Roger used, and it took him
a couple of minutes to take it in. "Oh. Grass. But, uh, why
pick on you?"

"I signed a petition about decriminalizing marijuana, which
incidentally I really believe should be done. I mean, God! the
things they do to those kids they find with a little dope.
Whereas L.B.J.—Well, anyway, I got in trouble down at
Stanford over the whole thing. Fortunately a kindly dean, a
woman, took care of me. But now I guess a lot of people think
I'm constantly stoned."

He laughed. "Well, are you?"

"Hardly. Honestly, I can't remember the last time I turned on."

However, as Roger glanced over he saw that she did remember. She was smiling to herself in a pleased, secret way—and looked very pretty as she did so, with those eyes.

Almost at Julia's door it occurred to Roger that it would have been nice to feed her, in some way. If not dinner at least a hamburger somewhere. And so he said, "I know I should have thought of this earlier, but is there a Zim's somewhere around? We could pick up a hamburger or something?"

Pausing, seeming to give this somewhat deeper thought than it deserved, Julia asked, "Do you like spaghetti? I could, uh, pull together some carbonara. Salad. There's some wine."

"Well, really, I don't want you to do all that." (But he did; it sounded terrific.)

"I'd like to. But how do you feel about garlic? That's a prime ingredient."

"I'm crazy about it."

In her narrow, unremodeled thirties kitchen, everything old and stained and creaking, in very little time Julia produced one of the nicest meals Roger ever had, he thought. Rich with butter and oil and Parmesan. Thick bacon, and indeed a lot of garlic. And a nice light crisp green salad. The burgundy was not too good, but what the hell, it was nice of her to go to all that trouble. Really nice.

Julia was a generous woman. Too generous for her own good, probably.

. . .

Her living room, to which they adjourned for coffee after dinner, was somewhat better: more narrow Victoriana, but some
nice exposed wood (Julia's handiwork). Shabby-comfortable
furniture, worn-down corduroy, old leather—and plants,
really too many plants. A philodendron so huge, climbing in
a corner of the room, that it looked tropical, dangerous. And
lots of ferns.

During dinner, they had talked mostly about each other's
marriages. Julia had been married twice—a small surprise,
that: Roger would have put her age at less than thirty. "Marriage doesn't seem to be something I'm very good at," she said,
in the slightly harsh, very wry style he later came to recognize
as hers.

And Roger admitted, "I was a lot at fault in my marriage,
God knows. It takes two to be wrong, don't you think?" He
still saw no point, though, in specific admissions (Candida, a
couple of her predecessors).

Now the conversation seemed to lag a little, possibly from
the sobering effects of coffee. Actually, Roger would as soon
have gone home just then, but to leave right after dinner
would have seemed impolite, if not downright ungrateful for
the meal.

Which one of them was it, then, who suggested that it
might be fun, or "interesting," to smoke a joint? It could have
been either, or both. In any case, from somewhere, some jar
or secret drawer, Julia brought out a couple of thin, misshapen
cigarettes. And lit them. And instructed. "Don't puff out.
Hold in as much as you can."

"It tastes funny," Roger told her a few minutes later, with a
little laugh.

And moments or maybe half an hour after that he said, "Did

you know that your philodendron could crawl? It's starting across the ceiling?"

This seemed very, very funny to them both. They laughed back and forth, contagiously, leaning toward each other and then starting up again. Until quite naturally they began to kiss, meeting somewhere halfway on the sofa.

Soon, or perhaps hours later, they were naked. Lights all out. They were making love, and for Roger the experience of Julia's body, then and always (quickly forgiven for voluptuous-ness), was like walking through rooms, a series, endless rooms, one after another. Walking, walking into explosions of light.

"I love you—"

"You're—"

"Beautiful, wonderful—"

"No, *you*—"

Those are the things they began to say to each other, Roger and Julia, that first night. As soon as they could talk.

The next morning, in Julia's cramped and lightless (but now magical) bedroom, Roger woke early. He had an appointment, he had to go home, shower and change.

He touched sleeping Julia, who woke and reached toward him, sleepily. Roger began to kiss her, soon found himself making love to her. Again.

Afterwards they both laughed, staring at each other. In disbelief. In the growing pale pre-dawn. "I'll see you tonight," Roger told her. "I'll call you."

"I'll be down at Stanford, and it's sort of hard to get me there. Just come over. Whenever."

.   .   .

All day, all through his appointments, driving about the city and during his few solitary hours at the drawing board, in a wondering way Roger thought, Good God, what have I fallen into? And he answered himself, Into love. This Julia is something else. *Marvelous.* Much more than I deserve.

He should bring her something. That was another thing in Roger's mind all day, some terrific present for Julia. Or at least he could call her and say he wanted to take her out to dinner. He couldn't have her cooking all the time. However, she had said it was hard to call her down there at Stanford.

He settled on some wine, a Napa cabernet that he knew to be reliable, if not superior. And a bunch of flowers, white narcissus that smelled of spring. Sweet. Aphrodisiac.

That night, within minutes of their collision at Julia's door, their ravenous kissing, they were in bed.

Somewhat later, Julia, in her pale-blue rather dowdy robe (that Roger found incredibly endearing, in a way that something more stylish never could have been)—Julia brought in glasses of wine, and one joint, which they shared. And then, after more wild and incredible love, she made dinner. A great stew that she had put together that morning, before driving down to Stanford.

In her kitchen, in her old robe, Julia moved with a sort of vagueness that Roger found extremely touching. His wife had been a dynamo of organization, and so was Candida. Julia seemed not to have the proper tool for any given task, and most of her knives were dull. But what she produced was somehow really, really good. (Except for the few things she forgot about and burned.)

Maybe, someday, he would remodel her kitchen for her. Roger thought of that, he imagined Julia in the big generous kitchen that she deserved: all wood, as he saw it, lovely soft grains of wood everywhere, and everything she needed near at hand, a large open rack of all the proper kitchen tools. And Julia there in a heavy dark red silk robe.

He could not resist telling her about this fantasy, tactfully leaving out the detail of the robe.

And Julia in her turn was deeply touched. Her wide amber eyes teared. "That's really lovely of you," she told him. "To imagine a kitchen for me."

"Someday I'll make it real," he promised.

Thus the pattern of their seeing each other was more or less established. Food and love, along with wine and joints. At Julia's house. Every night.

At times it did occur to Roger that this arrangement was unfair to Julia; he should take her out. God, the city was full of great restaurants, famous food. However, his divorce had made him more than a little edgy over money, and also, whenever he suggested to Julia that she might prefer going out, she protested that she loved cooking for him, loved the nest they had made of her house.

Roger tried to make up for these occasional twinges of guilt toward her by presents of wine and flowers, a lot of both, which Julia loved, she thanked and thanked him. Even, more practically, he brought her some good kitchen implements, a lemon zester, a decent potato masher. A set of knives.

And gradually they did begin to go out from time to time, mostly to neighborhood restaurants that Julia knew about.

A serious problem for Roger, though, as spring became summer and all this had been going on for a couple of months, was the fact that although he still loved Julia—madly, he really adored her—sometimes he just didn't want to drive to Twin Peaks that night. To see her. He would rather have been doing something else, even just seeing some guy from his office. Or doing nothing. Just for a change.

He managed to say a little of this to Julia. "Maybe we need a little time off from each other sometimes. You must have work, even old pals you want to see." (It had been tacitly acknowledged, then laughingly admitted, that their two sets of friends would quite possibly not get along.) To Roger's relief Julia quite agreed. "I should spend more time with women I know," she told him seriously. "That's good, your idea." And so they began to take off a few nights from time to time. In their separate but innocent pursuits.

Those sixties years were hard on middle-aged men, though. Making this observation, Roger further thought that it was especially true in warm weather. Young girls were everywhere with dresses up to there, and the longest, thinnest legs, lightly tanned. And breasts: so many girls going braless. He saw the multiple, wonderfully various shapes of young breasts, everywhere.

Very distracting, even for a man seriously in love.

.   .   .

Julia rarely talked about her work to Roger; how could she? He didn't know or understand the first thing about higher mathematics. However, one day at work she called him in great excitement.

"I won this prize," she told him. "It's really incredible. It's not just the money, although that's really nice. But this could lead to—oh, almost anything."

"Baby, that's great. Super great. Listen, we really have to celebrate."

"Wonderful. And I might do something really out of character, like buy a new dress."

Let me choose it, Roger for an instant thought, but of course did not say to Julia.

During that day, which was fogbound and dark, windy, cold, the start of a true San Francisco summer, Roger remarked on and wondered at his own somewhat lowered spirits, which he did not believe attributable to the weather. But he was forced to recognize that they had a lot to do with the evening ahead.

Just what did he fear, he asked himself. That Julia would buy and wear a dress that was somehow wrong, unbecoming? He could not believe himself quite so superficial, and besides he and Julia together had discussed the fact that visual taste was not her strongest suit. She had a certain cavalier indifference to objects, including clothes. This was one of the things he loved in her, wasn't it?

The important fact about the evening was her award, Roger firmly told himself. Her voice had been so excited, warm and wonderful, true Julia. And "It could lead to almost anything," she had said. Roger had no idea in a literal way just what she could have meant: money? prestige? further prizes? (Could he conceivably be jealous? threatened?)

Into his mind there floated a newspaper photo of a Nobel Prize recipient, in bed, in Stockholm. In fact, two people in two beds, a man and his wife. And surely the woman, who was very dark and attractive, was a mathematician? However, as Roger's memory cleared he recalled that the actual recipient of the prize was the husband, not his wife.

Ironies all around, not lost on Roger.

Instead of a dress Julia had bought a black silk shirt, heavy, rich-looking. Very tailored. Matching pants, tapered, narrow. Both perfectly fitted to her. To Roger she looked new and strange—in fact sensational. Even before their long ritual embrace in her hallway Roger cried out, "You're so beautiful, this is your look." He breathed into her hair, "Oh, I love you!"

Julia laughed, in a mildly chiding way. "You mean I look a lot better than usual? I guess I do. Don't count on its being permanent, though," and she laughed again.

All in all, it was one of their most successful evenings out, as Roger was always later to remember. Julia, happy and successful—and beautiful, she really was, in the shimmer of black silk, with her bright-red (generous, sexy) mouth. The scars were hardly visible. Judging her as objectively as he could, Roger saw what he had to recognize as style. Julia had hit on her own style; if she so chose she could go on, stylishly.

And Roger's fantasies about their life together began to expand, there in the excellently appointed, rather trendy new restaurant. With smart-looking Julia across from him. There was really no reason for them always to see each other in such cloistered, such entirely closed-in circumstances as had been their habit, Roger thought. For a while, of course, they had simply not wanted any interference with their miraculous privacy. Their exclusive passion. However, couldn't they now, conceivably, have both? Time for love alone and still, occasionally, other people? Possibly even develop some mutual friends, a small social circle of their own?

This did not seem the moment, though, for such a suggestion. Julia, who of course was exceptionally bright, and whose tongue could be sharp, might easily have countered, "You mean, now that I'm so well dressed we can start going out?" Which, even as a semi-joke, would be unfortunate.

Instead he told her, "This afternoon I had a fantasy about you winning the Nobel Prize. We were in bed together in Stockholm."

And Julia smiled, most beautifully. A successful happy woman, on the brink of her life.

Soon after that they went back to Julia's Twin Peaks aerie, and opened champagne and smoked dope and made love. Crazily. Fantastically. For hours.

Quite possibly it was their greatest night.

Why, then, when out of the blue a few days later (or, rather, the gray; it was still very cold and dark) Candida called, and in her old teasing voice, a little plaintive, saying she missed him, wanted to see him—why did Roger say, "Well, sure," not mentioning Julia?

Ah, fortunate, clever young Candida. Even the weather for her especial benefit seemed to break that day. The wind died down, the fog lifted, and there was a clean blue day, perfect for lunch on the docks at San Rafael, an old haunt of theirs.

Perfect for Candida's very short yellow linen dress.

"You look like a butterfly," Roger told her.

"Oh, you're always so mean to me, you never take me seriously."

Roger laughed at her, he always did. "What do you want me to say, you look like a tennis pro?"

"Oh, you're quite horrible. I can't think why I called you."

That was how they had always been together, very silly indeed, and somewhat sexy. And even while admitting to himself that Candida was silly, that together they made a fatuous dialogue, at the same time Roger thought, Well, why not? Do I have to be so intense and heavy all the time? Candida makes me feel young. My Candy.

As they left the table, Candida stood beside him for a moment, almost as tall as he, her lips just grazing his ear as she whispered (an old trick of hers but still rather sexy), "I suppose now you're going to whisk me off to some terrible motel."

What else could he say except, "I suppose I am," which is what he did say.

Making love to Candida (and the operative word was "to," whereas with Julia he made love with) was a somewhat more demanding process than he had remembered. For her pleasure, certain gestures must be prolonged, prolonged—as, though her intentions were probably generous, she did rather little in return. (Unlike Julia, giving everything, every time.)

But for most of the afternoon with Candida he managed not to think of Julia at all.

In those years, along with new notions of styles in hair and dress, messages of love were emanating from the young, the hippies. Make love not war, and love is all we need, and why don't we do it in the road? Or why not just make love with anyone, anywhere? Sexual freedom, and Roger, along with thousands of other older folk, thought the kids were obviously on to something, though of course they went too far. But people should make love more or less when they felt like it. Whenever, with whoever.

Naturally, Roger, on the whole a sensible person, would not have carried this message to some foolish extreme, nothing excessive like trying to make it with those really young girls, available though they all looked.

He did feel, though, that his continuing to see (to make love to, that is) both Julia and, on a far more occasional basis, Candida was culturally sanctioned, as it were.

It was even acknowledged between Roger and Candida that they both "saw" other people. Having more or less fallen in with the spirit of the times, or perhaps adapted it to her needs and/or convenience, Candida thought their "relationship" was "cool." "Of course being with you is the greatest, Roger, but in another way so is an afternoon sometimes with some other guy. My tennis instructor. After all, we only get one ride on this merry-go-round. Only impossible Edwin wouldn't get it." Edwin, husband of Candida, was ill-tempered, red-faced, and very rich.

At times, hours that he had to see as far-out flights of fantasy, Roger wished that he and Julia could have the same sort of free exchange, but of course that was crazy. Julia? NEVER.

In fact, in those days Julia was very caught up in her anti-war activity: meetings with other pacifist scientists, meetings with women for peace. Meetings with people with whom she most definitely did not go to bed.

And actually Julia's activism was one more thing for Roger to admire in her (Roger was a non-activist liberal). To admire and love. He *loved* her.

. . .

These days, partly because of Julia's many meetings, Roger and Julia were seeing each other two or three times a week. And in some very subtle, complex way, the intensity between them had very slightly diminished. One might have thought (Roger might have thought) that seeing each other less would have an opposite effect, that when they did see each other, after small lapses of time, they would fall upon each other as ravenously as in the early stages of their romance.

Over the months that they had been together, Roger knew that he had, in a way, tended not quite to look at Julia; he had taken her warm, sometimes moody, often passionate presence for granted. But sometime in the balmy fall that succeeded cold August he began to notice certain changes in her. For one thing she had lost weight, her body was leaner—to Roger, even sexier. But she also seemed to smile less, her face in repose was often sad, anxious-looking. Maybe the weight loss had this effect, giving her a somewhat drawn look?

Or maybe she was sad about Vietnam? the bombing of Cambodia?

One October morning Julia telephoned him at the office, again with what she said was great good news. But Roger took note of the fact that her voice did not sound happy, really.

Anyway, "We'll have to celebrate," he told her. "Even if you won't tell me yet what it is. Dinner out?"

For the moment he had forgotten that he was to have lunch with Candida, again in San Rafael. He thought of breaking the date, but then he further thought, Well, why? I can always tell Julia I'm tired, have to get up early. Something. (Innate fastidiousness had so far prevented his making love to both Candida and Julia on the same day.)

He arrived at her door with flowers, a great burst of white chrysanthemums, his car had been full of their slightly acrid, fall smell. And there was Julia, again in her rich black silk. She looked terrific. How could he ever have thought her less than good-looking? (And how he wished, just then, that he had not spent the afternoon with Candida in their motel.)

"You look fantastic," he told her after their kiss. "Tell me your news! Darling, you're always so reluctant—"

She smiled, but was it slightly wan, her smile?—the least shade guarded? "It's Berkeley," she told him. "They want me there. More rank, more money. It's actually quite incredible—"

Involuntarily thinking, Good, a move to Berkeley, she can get a nicer place, I'll help her with it and we can see each other on weekends—thinking all that even as he kissed her, Roger heard himself saying, "Baby, that's fantastic."

In the harsh porch light, as they headed out and toward his car, it seemed to Roger that Julia's facial scars looked deeper, suddenly, more prominent. Perhaps she was trying some new makeup that didn't work very well? Or maybe, perversely, losing weight deepened scars?

After helping her into her side of his car, Roger was aware as he came around to the driver's seat that for some reason she had switched on a light. He got in, saw her staring at a scrap of paper, yellow. Her face was frozen in an expression he had never seen.

And then, turning fully toward him, she spoke very loudly and clearly. "You rotten bastard!" she said. "Goddam you!"

Before Roger could take in what she had said, she had slammed out of the car and rushed off. Out, away.

Picking up the yellow paper, he saw indeed just what it was: the receipt for his afternoon's motel, and he thought, How on earth? I would never have left it there. *Candida!* On purpose! Fucking bitch, goddam *her.*

At that moment came the sound of Julia's old car, from across the street. Starting up, heading off.

No point even in trying to follow her. In Julia's mood, or for that matter in his own, they would only shout at each other, ruining everything. Besides, he was really tired.

The next day, Roger tried to call her down at Stanford, with no success. And that night at her house: no answer. He considered driving over there, up to Twin Peaks, but decided that she might well have gone to stay with friends.

Or if she was at home she was no more apt to answer the doorbell than the telephone.

Sending flowers did not seem quite the right gesture, somehow.

A few nights later, though, she did answer her phone. Indeed, in a very calm way she seemed to have been expecting his call. As well she might have been.

"You know, for quite a while I've had this idea that you were seeing someone else," she told him. "No real reason, I just thought that. But I so much wanted it not to be true. I convinced myself that I was being crazy. Delusional jealousy, I really accused myself. I guess you could call it denial, because I really knew. Don't ask me how, we were just too close for me not to. And then there it was. Concretely." Her voice, though still fairly calm and controlled, then rose as she said, "Jesus, Roger, how could you? So sleazy—"

No way to deny his guilt, and so Roger improvised. "I guess I sort of knew you knew, and I thought maybe you didn't mind," he lied. "You could have even been seeing someone yourself, some nice lefty physicist you met at meetings."

"Oh *shit*. You did not think that. You know me."

"Well, maybe I didn't really think it. Maybe I just hoped it." Possibly honesty could win her back at last? "But couldn't I see you? Could we at least talk?"

"We are talking. And no, I don't want to see you."

"But—"

"Please, Roger. I'm busy." Her voice now high and tremulous.

"But I love you." And never so much as now, he wanted to say, but it sounded silly. Not what she would have wanted to hear. And so he simply repeated, "I love you."

"You love *you*. Roger, goodbye."

Several times after that Roger called her, in the hours and days and weeks to come. But Julia always hung up, and Roger came to see that she meant it, she would have no more of him.

Unhappily, at just that time, that November, Candida was in Italy, touring with Edwin. And almost everyone else that Roger knew seemed similarly missing.

And, in the suddenly changing weather—an early, cold winter was generally predicted—all the girls with their visible legs and breasts seemed now to have taken cover. They were not around anymore, they may have migrated south to Mexico, like birds, or butterflies.

Thus, Roger thought even more obsessively than he might have, at the end of a love affair, of Julia. He felt as wounded as a schoolboy, and in an adolescent way he was pained by songs that brought her back. The Beatles singing "Lucy in the Sky with Diamonds," such a wonderful, perfect stoned song that he and Julia had listened to, laughing and very stoned.

Or "The Shadow of Your Smile." Except that he could not accurately, vividly remember Julia's smile. In fact, for an exceptionally visual person, he had considerable trouble seeing her at all. And when he did, instead of her smile or even her golden eyes he saw scars. Deep, irremediable scars.

WHAT TO WEAR

Thin and cold, although the San Francisco day is balmy, Sheila Cullan stands naked in her narrow, book-lined bedroom, arms crossed over her chest, paralyzed with indecision—she does not know what to wear. And the question is not frivolous; for Sheila, who teaches Victorian literature at a local university, it has metaphysical implications. Her lover is in the psychiatric ward of a local hospital, and she is going to see him, her first visit (quite possibly first and last).

In a year of knowing Braxton, Sheila has never known what might please him, might make him laugh, might interest or infuriate him, and the effort of trying has worn her out, or nearly.

And now, gone certifiably mad (she assumes he is mad, since he is there, locked up), he will be even more unpredictable, probably. How could she know what to wear, to visit Brax?

A sweater and jeans, running shoes? That is what Sheila usually wears when she is at home alone; it is what she feels most comfortable, most herself in. For teaching she wears shirts and skirts, hose, pumps. And at night for Brax she has been wearing whatever she thought he might like. (And she knows, Sheila has always known, the "incorrectness" as well as the total folly of her efforts.)

In terms of this hospital visit, what to wear to the ward, there is also the fact that most of the people in Psychiatric will be "lower income," often meaning no income at all. (Sheila's information comes mostly from a social worker friend, Maxine. Maxine, who never liked Brax, has also said, with some malice, "Brax is not going to like it there.") In any case, shy Sheila, who is hardly rich, does not want to appear conspicuously middle-class.

With long straight streaky brown hair, small and thin, Sheila looks younger than she is, almost thirty—and a lot younger than Brax, who is in his middle forties, still good-looking but overweight. Her youth and her thinness were always among her positive qualities for Brax, Sheila knows.

In his palmiest days, Brax was a high-flying real-estate operator in Marin; clothes were very important in his work, in his life. He always wanted Sheila really gussied up, as he liked to put it—in silks and her highest heels—when they went out to certain parties, openings, new restaurants.

But will this new Brax, someone quite sick, maybe really broken down—will this new person wish them both to be inconspicuous, in the ward? In that case, jeans and her old gray sweater would be just right.

How stupid, though, to stand there naked, deciding what to wear. How Brax would laugh, if he knew. How anyone would laugh, and think her a fool.

.   .   .

Once, and really by accident, Sheila managed to please Brax immensely with clothes. He was coming for dinner and, after cooking all afternoon, worrying more about whether he would like the chicken than what she would wear, Sheila at the last minute pulled out of her closet a long red dress, bought on sale the summer before (in her pre-Brax days Sheila bought clothes with more bravado). And he loved her in that dress. "Baby, you're gorgeous. Stick with red, it's your color."

The dinner itself was less of a success, and Brax was less enthusiastic about all the subsequent red clothes that Sheila bought; still, there had been that moment of triumph, that unforgettable "Baby, you're gorgeous."

Ironically, the psycho ward is only about five blocks from Sheila's apartment, ironic in that at last Brax is anchored somewhere near her. At least she knows where he is, which has not always been true; for the past month Brax has been defined as "missing."

This is what happened.

He was scheduled to have fairly routine surgery, a hernia, at Marin General Hospital. Scheduled some months in advance because, one, his internist saw no urgency; and, two, the surgeon of choice was vacationing in New Zealand.

Braxton talked a great deal about his coming operation, in what seemed to Sheila an obsessive, even exaggerated way. He referred to the event as the Grand Opening, along with more bad jokes of that nature. He drank even more than he usually did, and he did more coke. (Sheila *thought* he was doing more coke, that not being something they shared; Sheila is squeamish, drug-wise, partly because of an acid-trip brain-damaged older brother.)

This pre-operative period was a little tiresome, then, what with so many bad jokes, and so many drunken evenings.

At other times, though, Sheila berated herself for a lack of sympathy. She has never had surgery of any kind, and she too would find it frightening, she knew. Braxton was obviously "dealing with it" in his own available ways, which were not necessarily hers.

And then Brax vanished. First, he did not show up one night when he was to take her out to dinner, and it was not just an ordinary going-out plan: they were to cruise around the bay in some hotshot client's boat, and then a very late dinner in town. Braxton was often late, but on the other hand that boat arrangement involved other people and a specific time, 7:30, to meet at the pier.

Sheila knew better than to try to read, waiting for Brax. It was better to putter about, to involve herself in very small, marginally useful tasks. She sewed on a button, she polished two small coffee spoons and a pair of silver earrings. She washed off the shelf on which she kept salad oils, and then ate some yogurt, seated alone at her round wooden kitchen table. In her new summer black Go-Silk.

By nine she thought, Well, he's not coming—could he have gone ahead without me? Deciding that I would not especially get along with the big hot client? Well, he knew that in the first place, he's always known that. There'll be some drunken phone call at 3 a.m. to explain, Sheila thought, which is what had happened on the only other occasion of Brax not showing up.

But there was no 3 a.m. call from Braxton, nor calls at any other time. The next day, a Saturday, Sheila suffered a miserable combination of sleeplessness and anxiety. She went out for several short walks, in the cool sweet early May air, but came home to no messages on her answering machine. At last, late in the afternoon, most reluctantly she called his office, although one of the things she was thinking was, This is useless, whatever's going on they'll cover for him.

However, one of the younger salesmen answered, a man whom Sheila had met and sort of liked (he was trying out real estate to help him write his novel; he would not last, Braxton had thought). "We haven't heard a thing," this young man now told Sheila. "He stood those people up last night, which is not like Brax, and then he didn't show up today. No answer at his place. I was worried, I was going to call you. Could he have taken a powder, as they used to say?"

"I don't know, I guess he could have."

He could indeed have run off to avoid the operation, was one of Sheila's thoughts. Or to avoid his work, which most of the time he hated. And very likely, in a way, to avoid her too. He could have just run off, period. Or he could have gotten really high and jumped off some bridge.

The weeks that followed were for Sheila a strange and mostly terrible time. Fortunately she was extremely busy just then with papers, finals, clearing up the sheer detritus of the academic year, but she still had a large amount of pure anxiety time, hours during which she experienced every variety of fear for Brax, for large florid handsome old Brax, whom, despite all indications that she should not do so, she truly loved.

She also experienced certain fears of Brax: a dread that he might at some dark hour arrive to lean on her doorbell, drunk and angry. He had done just that one night, early on in their connection (one of the times that she should have left him, for good).

There were even some hours during which she experienced a certain relief at his absence, relief from a connection that was violent and exciting and more than a little crazy. Brax was someone quite apart from what Sheila saw as her real life, from what she perceived as reality: her job and her students, books and friends. Brax was the demon lover from whom sooner or later, in one way or another, she knew she would have to part.

And then two days ago came the call from the hospital. "We have a Mr. Braxton Dunbar in the psychiatric ward. He would like to see you. Visiting hours on Sunday start at two."

Sheila was vastly relieved, of course—and terrified.

And here it is, a bright June Sunday, and Sheila is still standing naked in her bedroom, torn with impossible conflict over the seemingly idle question (although with Braxton nothing was ever idle) of what to wear. And visiting hours will begin in thirty minutes.

Sheila's apartment consists of the upper floor of a narrow Victorian house in a block of very similar houses. A medium-good neighborhood on the outskirts of expensive Pacific Heights. The sidewalks on Sheila's block are in serious disrepair; sturdy trees with massive roots have cracked and broken through the concrete. Those trees provide the block with considerable charm, though; it was mainly for the trees that Sheila, from Oregon and used to trees, first rented this place. She has always meant to find out what kind of trees these particular ones are, but so far has not. She admires their tenacious strength, however; she is awed by those powerful roots. She especially likes the trees' leafed-out summer look; just now they are all feathery, pale green.

Looking out at the trees, in the sunlight, Sheila experiences a small jolt of pleasure, perhaps even of strength. How very pretty they are! What a nice place to live, after all. And in that happier instant she sees clearly what she should wear to visit Brax, stupid not to have thought of it before. She will wear a new pink silk blouse, bought on sale out on Sacramento Street to cheer herself up, in that long time of hearing nothing from Brax. Of course she should wear it, the blouse is something he has not seen, no associations to any of their troubled history together. And a pricey blouse, even on sale; Brax, who is something of a clothes snob, will recognize its quality. And the blouse is becoming, she knows it is—the famous flattery of pink.

Maxine the social worker has made it clear that you do not take presents, or not the usual hospital offerings, candy and flowers, to the psychiatric ward. And Brax does not read. And so (Sheila hopes this will happen) he might see this offering of herself in something new and "good" as a sort of present.

How Brax himself will actually be is an issue that Sheila is simply not facing. She knows that.

Dressed and standing outside, Sheila again appreciates the trees, and indeed the general pleasantness of her block, the clean bright white paint on the Victorian curlicues of a shining dark blue house, and a bricked-in garden that she especially admires: a profusion of white petunias and baby's breath, some California poppies, and some small climbing old-fashioned white roses, on a lattice.

So admirable, this gardening impulse, Sheila believes, contributing as it does to the neighborhood and to the pleasure of passing strangers—a positive human instinct to give, to do good. She can even equate this urge with her own wish to look well, visiting poor Brax in the psycho ward.

But while she walks and thinks that phrase, "Brax in the psycho ward," her small self-congratulatory mood dissolves as she demands (of no one), What will he be like?

She has no clue at all, no one has told her anything about his state, nor why he is there. She has only past performance to go on, and that includes almost everything. Affection, abuse, and humor. Exuberance, despair. Passion and coldness. Brax has shown all those things; he could now be in almost any phase, or possibly a new one.

Sheila is only quite sure that he will hate being where he is. The fact that he hasn't somehow escaped is amazing—assuming that he has not, that he will in fact be there this afternoon. But proud, rebellious Brax in a common psychiatric ward, with common crazies? He will hate it there, and will this hatred extend itself to visitors, to those outside and free, and presumably okay? Sheila is suddenly convinced that this will be true. He will think, How dare she show up looking perfectly well, in her clearly expensive new clothes?

So sure is she of this idea of Brax that Sheila stops where she is, two blocks from the hospital (and three from her apartment), in a neighborhood far less appealing than her own, with shabbier, untrimmed houses, no sidewalk trees. She stops and turns around and begins to hurry home.

To change her clothes.

She has raced along the street, and now she rushes through the act of changing, as though performing some propitiatory task in which speed is one of the requirements. Out of the new pink silk and into the old gray Shetland, out of good black linen pants and into jeans and worn blue runners. And, re-dressed and outside again, she hurries along the five blocks to the hospital. As she does so, she tells herself that it doesn't matter, she does not have to get there at the start of Visiting, necessarily. But she is unable to stop this rush, this racing in Braxton's direction.

His ward is in a building across the street from the main hospital (more Maxine information). Sheila goes up a ramp and swings through glass doors. Two fair beefy guards (maybe twins?) sit behind a desk; one of them instructs her to sign in. Sheila does so, half wondering as she writes what happens if you forget to sign out. Do they find you and lock you up with the crazies, where you probably belonged in the first place?

In the elevator she pushes the proper button, the ascent begins, and only then does Sheila recognize how acutely frightened she is.

Too late to go back, however. Doors open, and there she is, confronting another desk. This time a pleasant-faced, dark-haired nurse instructs her to sign in. There are two baskets of floral "arrangements" on the desk, and Sheila thinks, Oh, I really could have brought something, but there again, too late.

"He's down the hall, I think. You'll see him" is what the nurse has said, and so Sheila starts down the hall.

People. She passes a pretty, thin black woman in perfectly ordinary daytime clothes: a patient? nurse? social worker? A room where five or six men are smoking and watching some game on TV. An old-looking woman with long gray curls, wearing a tattered pink chenille robe and muttering to her-self—clearly a patient.

She has almost reached the windows at the end, and has almost thought, with a wild surge of what must be relief, Oh, he's not here after all, when she sees that the man standing there, standing against the light and thus very hard at first to see—that man is Braxton.

"Hi," he says. "I see you made it."

"Oh, yes." And then, unavoidably, "Well, how are you?"

During this interchange, they have moved together and then apart for the lightest, most fleeting embrace. But even in that brief touch, Sheila has thought, How thin he is, down to bones.

And now, standing back as she looks at him, she sees that he is indeed very thin. Diminished. His old clothes hang on him.

Thin was a condition she had surely not expected. Sheila has hitherto thought of madness as enlarging: Lear, Mrs. Rochester. Recognizing this useless preconception, she begins to fight tears of pity, compassion, maybe—for poor thin Brax, tears of sheer sadness at his diminution.

"I've lost a lot of weight," Brax tells her. "I was up at Tahoe and I got sick and had to go off the sauce, but shit, Sheila, it's nothing to cry about."

"I'm not. I'm sorry, but I have been sort of worried."

He looks at her fiercely, pale-blue eyes now larger in his much less fleshy face—and wild. He asks her, "Is that why you got so dressed up to come to see me? Stunning outfit, kid. Love that gray sweater."

His tone is so brutally familiar—always, he has bludgeoned her with this heavy irony—that, reeling, Sheila thinks, But he's really just the same. Has he always been mad?

She would like to ask him what he did that put him there, what act, at last. She decides against asking him anything, though.

Brax says, into their silence, "Same old guy, only worse— is that right?"

I've got to get out of here, Sheila thinks, even as she is

asking, "Is there anything I could bring you? You know, just five blocks—"

Leaning down to her, he begins to whisper: "You don't have to bother, I'm cutting out of here tomorrow. An old buddy of mine is sailing me down to Mexico." And then he says, "Of course he may not show. And in that case—" He looks at her appraisingly, calculating. "If you do come back, wear red, okay? I've got my standing in this place to think about."

Shortly after that, not remembering quite how she left, nor whether or not she signed out, Sheila is walking home. But she is disoriented, uncertain even of the familiar direction. She stumbles on a broken piece of sidewalk, and barely recovers her balance.

People end up in psychiatric wards for all sorts of reasons, she tells herself, not all of them valid. And so, although she would still like to know, it almost doesn't matter why Brax is there.

She should not go to see him again, though, if a single encounter can make her stumble along the street, and can make her see, as now she does, brutal messages in the hieroglyphic graffiti scrawled on a green post-deposit box.

However, the sudden thinness could mean he is truly ill, needing help?

In any case, if she does go to see him again (if he has not after all got away to Mexico), Sheila thinks, At least I will know what to wear.

TRAVELING TOGETHER

A few years ago, in a relentlessly remodeled hotel in Milan, near La Scala, a young American woman experienced a time of quite unbelievable panic. Susan Quince, a dean in a small women's college, just arrived in Italy with her lover, at that black pre-dawn hour felt panic as acute and as absolute as it was irrational, worse and more frightening than anything since the terrors of early childhood, which Susan no longer remembered. For that horrifying hour or so in Milan, she believed that she was no longer subject to the reassuring pull of gravity; at any moment she might slip out into space, into blackness. Infinity. Hell.

So powerful was her delusion that she clutched the sheets, knowing as she did so that nothing would work, she would fall away, herself as flimsy as linen sheets. It was odd, she later thought, that she did not grasp the bedframe; she may have believed that the bed would go too, sailing out into night. A child's nightmare.

Nor, as she might have done, did she reach for and grip the arm or the shoulder of Ralph Truitt, her lover—a Los

Angeles doctor, an internist, with whom she was traveling—then.

Least of all did Susan do anything as sensible as going into the bathroom and turning on the light, and finding out the time, a clear fact. Maybe taking a pill of some sort. Even in that strange hotel she could have found the right door—to what she later recalled as an especially ugly room, all glaring bright-red tile, heavy threatening chrome.

She simply lay there in terror, having (she felt) no relationship to the earth, no roots, no worldly weight. And entirely convinced of the reality of her own sensations.

As she thought, This trip is a serious mistake. We should surely have canceled.

And indeed, they had quarreled horrendously during the week just preceding this trip; they had meant to call it off. But at last they decided to go to Italy *anyway,* saying such things to each other as, We usually have fun on trips. And, It's just a trip we're taking, it doesn't commit us to anything further along (they had earlier talked about moving in together, even of marriage).

None of those things were entirely true, though. They had not always had fun on trips; last summer in England was not a total success, nor was the Dordogne, the spring of their first knowing each other. And the fact of going off to Italy together, their third trip, did have at least an air of commitment. Certainly it was giving themselves another chance.

Quite possibly they were simply too tired, too stressed-out from the fighting to go through all the business of cancellations, making other vacation plans for that particular week in May that they had both, with considerable trouble, arranged to take off. Taking the trip was taking the easy way out.

Certainly both of them, Dean Susan and Ralph the doctor, recognized the seriousness of their quarrel. They were shocked by their own violence, the ugliness of what they said to each other.

The fight. Its simple cause was that Ralph had not shown up at a small but "important" party given by Susan, at her college, the college being an hour or so by freeway out of Los Angeles, where Ralph's hospital and his small apartment were. Whether Ralph had entirely forgotten the party or simply confused the date was an issue somehow obscured in the subsequent heat; it began not to matter. In any case, Susan's party was to honor a visiting sculptor, a distinguished elderly woman (does Ralph basically not like or even recognize distinction in women? So many questions arose, all of them unpleasant in their implications). Mid-party, or somewhat earlier, fearing freeway trouble or medical emergencies, Susan telephoned his apartment—and was answered quite cheerily (indeed somewhat drunkenly, Susan thought) by Ralph himself, with a sexy sound of Brazilian music in the background.

And so it began.

Ralph: "No, in fact I was not alone. I'd asked Mrs. Harris—you remember June?—to come by for a drink, we'd been in the O.R. all day and she looked beat, and her husband's very sick. And no, in point of fact I did not have sex with her. But even if I had, is that the end of the world?"

Susan: "But how could you forget? You knew how important it was to me, I kept telling you. Don't you care—don't you listen?"

And so on.

For Ralph the central issue became Susan's alleged sexual jealousy, her suspicions; that is what he talked about. And Susan, not admitting this to him (she still argued simply that he should have come to her party), in her heart or in some other intensely vulnerable interior place knew he was right, in part. She did worry about Ralph and nurses, about vigorous attractive Ralph, an hour away, with almost anyone. Patients, even.

Unholy passions flared.

At times Susan thought that he must indeed have had sex, as he put it, with June Harris, else why should he be so defensive over his rights to sexual freedom? Hard to believe that his ardor was abstract, defense of a principle. Susan never quite made that accusation; after all, he kept making it himself.

And Ralph thought, and he did say, that Susan made too much of a simple party, which had gone off perfectly well without him, hadn't it? Of course he was sorry, he did know she had counted on his being there. However, surely she knows by now what a doctor's life is like? The impossibility of planning ahead?

And now, for God's sake, what should they do about Italy?

Well, what the hell, they actually might as well go. Lord knows they could use a rest. They were both too worn down to think of another solution, for anything.

On the morning after her hours of panic, to her great surprise Susan felt much better, better than she would have believed, in view of the night before. Clearly, despite that horrifying delusional hour, she had managed at last to go back to sleep, and had awakened refreshed, barely able to recall the nature of her fear, or its shape. Certainly she did not mention or try to describe it to Ralph, who tended to be intolerant of what he deemed irrational.

"I know, I'll bet you're hungry," he said as Susan emerged all clean and almost dressed from the garish bathroom. "Well, you're in luck, so am I. I'll hurry and shave."

A problem on other trips had been Susan's waking hungers, since Ralph often liked a good long exploratory walk before breakfast. Susan also wanted an earlier dinner than he did, Ralph liked a long drinking hour. At one point he had even suggested that Susan get her blood sugar checked, there might be some problem. But so far Susan had not, she was sure that whatever problem there was existed only in her head.

Deciding against the hotel dining room, they found a nice open café just a couple of blocks away, in the direction of the Galleria, which was where they had meant to go. Excellent coffee, wonderful fresh rolls. Even fresh orange juice.

"How'd you sleep?" Ralph asked her.

"Pretty well, considering the trip, time zones and everything. I did wake up for a while, but then I must have gone back to sleep."

"I must say, you did really well on the flight."

On the first trips, Susan had been an extremely frightened flier, white-knuckled, convinced that any turbulence meant crashing, death. She had been so uncomfortable flying that prior to this trip, which she had wanted to be successful, she took a small seminar for scared fliers. A modest group who met intensively, five nights a week for two weeks, and who were asked by their leader, a mousy-looking but very assured young man, to visualize and then describe the worst of their fears. Susan hated every moment of those sessions; she regarded both the leader and the other students (mostly salesmen, forced to travel) with distaste. It was rather like flying itself, she observed: too much time spent too closely among people whom you did not choose.

However, on this trip, once she and Ralph were on the plane in Los Angeles, strapped in and ready, Susan recognized that she was indeed much better. Not feeling her customary panic.

And she noticed (she thought) a certain disappointment on

Ralph's part. He kept on looking at her in an inquiring, ostensibly sympathetic way; *was* she all right, during the rough moments of ascension through thick dark covering clouds? She was, she smiled to reassure him, but found on his face an expression that was ambiguous.

Congratulating her bravery, though, Ralph at least sounded sincere—and perhaps everything, or at least most things, would work out well on this trip?

Later, Susan was to remember Milan less as the scene of her overwhelming, wild attack of panic (fortunately she thought very rarely of that seizure) than as the place where all the shoes were: thousands, millions of shoes, in every shopwindow. And not just ordinary shoes, but rather very, very high-style shoes: that year high thin heels and pointy toes, in a gaudy spectrum of exotic colors—jungle greens, plumage scarlets, and wild bright pinks. In silks and suèdes and every type of scaly skins. Entirely impractical shoes.

"What on earth do they do with all those shoes next year? They can't possibly sell them all." This from Susan to Ralph, at lunch.

"That bothers you?"

"Well, yes, actually it does. The sheer waste of it." Susan was sometimes called a bleeding heart by Ralph, but she kept on with it. "They're such evanescent shoes. You couldn't exactly give them to the homeless."

"Women should refuse to wear shoes like that in the first place," Ralph pronounced.

"Well, of course they should." Susan hoped this would not lead to a discussion of women's roles. "But think how long it would take for manufacturers to get the message," she added.

"Well, time for the Cathedral?" Ralph asked.

Our conversations never seem to last very long, Susan observed, with a small, interior sigh.

Bergamo. Ralph will remember this as the place where it was impossible to park, Susan thought as he nosed the small white rented Fiat up the narrow, sharp cobbled street to the already filled parking area for their hotel.

And I will remember it as the place with the narrowest, farthest-apart single beds yet, she thought a little later, Ralph having found, as he always did, a handy space, their laborious registration completed. I will remember it as another place where we did not make love, she (correctly) prophesied.

Twin beds. Accustomed to the canopied, carved-mahogany double bed of Susan's rather Victorian quarters, in her college, or to the king-sized mattress swathed in bold "designer" stripes of Ralph's bachelor pad, on Mulholland—or the queen- or king-sized super beds of motels in La Jolla and Santa Barbara, San Diego or Carmel—used to love on those broad, convenient spaces, to having each other's bodies near at hand, available, Ralph and Susan find themselves defeated, always, in terms of sex, by separate beds. Or so Susan has put it to herself.

But she has also thought that in most cases, Bergamo excepted, the beds were not actually insuperably far apart, nor (if you really wanted to be together) impossibly narrow.

In Verona, Susan and Ralph were given, again, a room with twin beds. However, they seemed to be up in a sort of turret, from which there was a lovely, winding view of the narrow river.

"Then we can't be far from the museum," Ralph told her. "It's on the river. And if we're lucky the restaurant could be around here too."

Ralph had been told by a much traveled, important medical colleague that both the museum and a certain restaurant are "absolute musts" in Verona. In fact for that reason, the colleague's insistence, they had veered from their course to Venice. "The game pie in that place is the absolute greatest," Ralph was told, a set of orders that he relayed to Susan.

The restaurant was indeed quite near their hotel: a dark-paneled upstairs room, not large, fairly crowded with small round tables whose dingy white linen cloths hung limply to the floor. And at 8:30, the hour of their reservation, no other customers. A small cluster of waiters lingered near a far, broad door, presumably leading to the kitchen.

"Good we reserved," said Susan, intending a small joke.

But Ralph was frowning. "I wonder if it could be the wrong place."

The waiter who arrived at their side assured them, though, that this was the correct, the internationally famous restaurant. And he led them to a table. "Early yet" was his parting shot, delivered with a crooked grin. He was fairly old, with a dragging limp.

"Well, the food had better be really terrific," Ralph warned, his words directed to the waiter's back.

"We could go somewhere else. It really doesn't look too great. You know, places change." This was generous of Susan, who was hungry, afflicted by blood sugar or perhaps the simple fatigue of travel. She felt certain, though, that the food would not be good, clearly not the memorable feast to which Ralph looked forward. And in his disappointment he would be angry, perhaps abusive—some bad familiar mood.

"No, I promised Bill we'd check it out." Ralph's tone was ominous, and Susan braced herself.

The first blow, delivered along with their Cinzanos, was the waiter's announcement that there was no game pie. "Famous specialty, but only in the fall. Season of the chase," he explained, as though they could not have figured that out for themselves, which of course they should have.

But "People do shoot birds in May," Ralph insisted, with his dark, aggressive scowl.

"No game pie." The waiter smiled widely, revealing gold, and a few black gaps.

"Well, you don't have to be so goddam pleased about it." Ralph's loud and terrible voice resonated in the empty room.

For a few minutes the two men simply stared at each other: large, dark, healthy, successful Ralph, who was disappointed, foiled in his immediate plans for game pie and subsequent boasts to Bill, his well-traveled and well-fed colleague; and the smaller, older, less healthy waiter, who was more or less accidentally in charge of the next hour or so of Ralph's life.

In the next instant Ralph would stand up and push the waiter aside. Susan gripped her napkin, waiting. He would pull her up and out of the restaurant.

But she was wrong. Icily, Ralph requested the menu; in a frozen silence he and Susan perused the fare while the waiter stood miserably by. They ordered soup and salad, veal for Ralph, for Susan chicken—with none of their usual food-ordering chatter.

Their waiter served each dish with a sort of meticulous contempt, whether for the food, which he must know to be inferior, or for Ralph and Susan—impossible to tell. Maybe

(Susan thought) he simply hated the situation in which he found himself, an old waiter in a restaurant that had gone very sharply downhill, serving bad food to rich, unpleasant foreigners.

By the time they were ready to leave, several other couples had arrived, and so it took a while to get their check. Insult to injury, for Ralph.

At last, though, check in hand, he stood up and faced the waiter, standing both too close and too far above him. "I would simply like you to know that this is the worst food we have encountered in all of Italy. It is a disgrace. Abominable." And Ralph peeled off a sheaf of lire, which he then thrust upon their table.

Barely waiting for Susan, he began to stalk from the room, so that she was considerably behind him, and able to hear the waiter in his wake: "Asshole American son of bitch."

The next morning in the museum, which was indeed a small marvel, most elegantly restored, and arranged, with its overlook of the river—the Ralph whom Susan liked and sometimes loved re-emerged. Following his eager, energetic back, his narrow, dark, intelligent head, Susan was drawn again to his greedy curiosity, his sharp appreciation of what he saw: sculpture and painting, architecture, and feats of engineering, in beautiful stone.

Still, as she thought of the night before she quailed, particularly as she thought of the waiter.

In fact, a few years later, by which time Susan had managed, at last, to sever ties with Ralph for good, she still sometimes thought of that waiter. She could always see his face very clearly—along with the shoes in the shops of Milan, all those beautiful useless colors.

Heading at last toward Venice on the following day, Susan thought in a general way about trips. Traveling tends to intensify whatever is good—or bad—in any relationship, was one of her conclusions. Two people, generally unaccustomed to spending that much time together, have fewer resources for getting away from each other, for breathing space.

On trips, a very fearful person may develop strange panics in the night.

And an angry person will become even angrier, off home ground. (Susan recognized that she was still trying to forgive Ralph's behavior with the waiter, and recognized too that a fearful person is often very forgiving.)

Venice. Their Venetian hotel room, as though to compensate for all other disappointing, less than beautiful rooms, was (though quite discreetly) perfect. Its balconied window looked out on a small canal, an arched bridge, a tiny park with a single tree, a pine. And the room's regally broad bed lay deep within a curtained, recessed alcove.

Their dinner too was superb (another, luckier recommendation from Bill, the traveling colleague). "This is really the greatest pasta I've ever had," Ralph pronounced, gazing about the gilt-and-marble room, then returning his look to the long windows adjacent to their table. The view of the brilliant, shadowed, mysterious Piazza San Marco. Across the way a bandstand, and a bright café. Wandering tourists, all of whom from this distance had an air of mystery, even of distinction.

"This is unreal," Ralph said to Susan, with his smile, across the flickering candlelight. "I don't believe it."

But did he mean Venice, or the fact that at last they were able to enjoy their trip? Susan was unsure—and she too had sometimes wondered which was the more real, the more significant: fights and trouble, or their occasional rapport, stray moments of love?

After dinner they walked slowly across the piazza to the café, where at small round tables groups of people, or some alone, took coffee in tiny cups, or rich liqueurs, or velvet-colored brandies. Getting into that spirit, festive, celebratory, Ralph and Susan ordered and drank Chartreuse—they drank several, in fact. Both the queer green-yellowish color and the exotic taste seemed perfectly right for that moment.

Having drunk too much, and later made love with a kind of anonymous violence, both Ralph and Susan woke up after a scant few hours of the thinnest sleep, both thirsty, both with incipient headaches. Dosing themselves with aspirin, drinking water, they went back to bed, where nevertheless they fell upon each other ravenously again. Like strangers, in a strange hotel.

The trip home began with a train from Venice to Milan, mostly through an impenetrable fog, so dense that Susan worried about their flight, that night: Milan–New York–Los Angeles.

Ralph reassured her. "Heavy fog over northern Italy does not mean a fog-covered Atlantic. Not necessarily."

As always, he sounded both reasonable and authoritative,

and Susan decided that (as always) she was worrying too much, foreseeing trouble that would very likely not take place.

But Ralph was wrong.

An hour out of Milan, aloft and heading westward above the Atlantic, the weather outside the windows of the plane looked fierce: dark huge ragged clouds, wind-torn.

And *turbulence*. The FASTEN SEAT BELT and NO SMOKING signs had never gone off, the giant plane began to be shaken like a toy, a rattle, in the monumental wind. Up and down, sideways, everything jolted and rattling.

Susan felt herself given over to panic, her breath and her heart all awry, all out of control. And nothing worked, no words of wisdom, no practical suggestions for dealing with fear.

Beside her, Ralph lifted her hand from the seat divider, which Susan was clutching. He held it firmly in his larger, stronger hand, smiling down at her.

And as her fingers now grasped at his, as she held to him, seemingly for dear life, somewhere in Susan's tossing, terrified mind was the thought: I can never leave him, I will never find the nerve.

YOUR DOCTOR LOVES YOU

After her husband, Sebastian, had left her, all alone in their beautiful, entirely impractical house (drafty, leaking, often cold and dark), Holly Jones felt loss as something sharp in the cavity of her chest. Her pain was severe, and in those terrible days, and weeks, then months, Holly, a basically friendly, chatty young woman, sought to ease that pain, somewhat, by talk. By trying to talk it out.

Those obsessive conversations went on continuously, like tapes. Some were entirely silent, going on in her head, and those were with—or, rather, to—Sebastian. Sebastian, a handsome, old-family-rich, non-violent alcoholic, often impotent—an unsuccessful though talented painter (so he and Holly thought)—had gone off to New York, it seemed for good. He often used to go there, on gallery or family business, but this time he had been gone for three months, during the last of which he had not communicated with Holly.

These Sebastian talks were a terrible mix of cold analysis and warm vituperation, often with more than a little scalding lust thrown in; Holly had always wanted Sebastian, she did still. But gradually she came to see that all this quiet talk to him, these silent screams did her no good, and she made a serious effort to stop all that. (And she called a lawyer.)

Her actual, voiced conversations were mostly with her friend Mary, a sculptor, a somewhat older and at least temporarily happier woman, married to a pediatrician. These real conversations were frequent; kindly Mary made a lot of time for Holly. And generally they were helpful, though sometimes not. Sometimes just a heavy dose of Sebastian-talk could throw Holly backward, into tears or worse, back into her wide unshared bed, in the lovely glassed-in bedroom that now, in January, was often freezing cold. In Ross, California, just north of San Francisco.

Occasionally, in a deliberate way, both Holly and Mary tried to shift the focus of their talk away from Sebastian and onto almost anything else: the weather, Reagan, the contras, the Democratic candidates. Clothes, old friends, gossip. Their friendship predated both marriages. It went back to the days when they lived in North Beach, in San Francisco, and were fairly broke, working at odd jobs. Holly, a leggy blonde, did mostly modeling while she took courses at the Art Institute; and Mary, who cooked in an Italian restaurant, also studied sculpture at the Institute. They had always liked each other, although "when I first met you I thought you were so pretty you had to be some kind of a bubble head," Mary had confessed. In stages, Mary first, both women had moved to Marin. With husbands. Their social lives had diverged (Sebastian did not much like Mary; as some men will, he suspected the "best friend" of sharing evil confidences concerning himself). But they still knew enough people in common to talk about.

One of the people they knew and mentioned from time to time was a man named Jonathan Green, Dr. Green, an internist in Mill Valley, to whom they both went as patients. Jonathan was tall and dark and heavy, a serious, kindly-looking man in his middle fifties (Sebastian's age). Even today, in Marin County, Jonathan made house calls; he seemed to care incredibly for his patients. Some time ago Mary had heard (through Mark, her husband) that Jonathan was getting a divorce.

And one morning, the day after her annual checkup with Jonathan, Mary remarked rather carelessly to Holly, "You know, I get the impression that Jonathan's really interested in you."

"Oh, come on."

"I really think so. You're all he talks about, he knows we're friends. He wanted to know if you felt better now. Really, Holly, he could be in love." She laughed. "Why not give it a whirl? Why not call him and ask him to dinner?"

"Oh. Well. Well, really, it seems so unlikely. I mean, I know Jonathan likes me, but I think he likes all his patients. Love! Honestly, Mary."

But Holly's heart, like an uncaged bird, had begun to soar into higher air as ancient, buried hopes revived.

Just suppose it were true, she thought. Just suppose. Jonathan Green. Well, why not? He was not as handsome or fun as Sebastian at his best could be, but on the other hand not an alcoholic, not vain or irresponsible or mean. A caring person, a man unlikely to hurt her. Someone serious. A doctor.

Indeed, why not ask him for dinner?

She telephoned Jonathan, one of whose virtues was phone-availability to patients. She heard his pleasant, soft, somewhat tentative voice almost right away. "Well, I hardly know what to say. How nice" was Jonathan's response.

But then a certain amount of trouble set in: finding an evening that would work out for them both. Jonathan was on call a lot, it seemed, he had a medical society meeting, an evening with his kids. Holly had only one date, with an old friend up from L.A. She never broke dates, although this time she was tempted. But at last a night was established, ten days off. Jonathan would come over to her house for dinner.

"It's too far off," Holly complained to Mary. "Too much time for me to think and get nervous. God, a date. I haven't had a date in ten years."

"You already sound better, though. It'll be good for you."

It was true that Holly felt better.

Married to Sebastian, she had always been aware of his acute, censorious, controlling eye. The look of the house could never be quite right, nor the meals. Nor, God knows, Holly's opinions. Unstated but heavily, coldly present was the fact that Holly had grown up in a trailer park near Tucson; her father was a Yugoslavian metalworker, a drunk, whose awful name, Jewerelsky, Holly had happily given up for Jones—and for Sebastian. Holly could thus not be expected to do things, anything, correctly, although Sebastian did expect things of her, actually. He expected everything.

However, there was no reason to believe that Jonathan Green was at all like that. A busy doctor, he might not even notice how his house looked, or not notice in the meticulous, cruel way that Sebastian did.

Holly went about in a happy flurry of straightening up, cleaning, and polishing. Even rearranging, putting a vase of flowers on the hearth, daring to remove a couple of Sebastian's paintings (stark steel girders, flying freeways), and substituting an old one of her own, of flowers.

. · .

Sebastian married Holly and bought this house on what now seemed (to Holly) a single impulse, a manic summer whim. "Oh, you're the prettiest girl in the world. You know what you are? You're cute, you're a living doll," he had crooned to her, that first summer (drunkenly, but you had to know Sebastian very well indeed to know when he was drunk. He "drank like a gentleman"). And "I'll have to buy you the prettiest house in Marin. It's all wonderful wood, all windows and skylights, and everything around it green, all flowing." And Holly, tipsy herself on champagne (she did not drink much and, according to Sebastian, did not know how), Holly was charmed into love with Sebastian, and later with the house.

Sebastian then was in his mid-forties, his dark blond handsomeness in its ripest phase. "My autumn," he said of himself, one long finger caressing the cleft in his chin. "If I grew a beard it would come out gray. You should have known me when I was young and gorgeous, baby doll."

"You're gorgeous enough. I mean, you're plenty gorgeous."

In those days she could usually make him laugh.

And Holly did fall in love with the house, along with Sebastian. It was a lovely summer house, built as such near the turn of the century by some San Francisco people seeking escape from the city's summer fog. There was a single, very large high-beamed room; as Sebastian said, all wood and windows and skylights. A small glassed-in bedroom to one side, surrounded by ancient, giant ferns and live oaks, cypress, manzanita. The house was a dream that Holly herself could have had, in the trailer, in the desert, a dream of hills and greenery, of polished wooden spaces, and no sand, anywhere, to sweep.

Lovingly, Sebastian chose all the furniture, their bed with

its intricate brass headboard was his especial pride, and the
track lights installed to illuminate his paintings. His house.
And for ten years Holly went along with all that, yielding to
his superior taste and wisdom. Wishing he would drink less
and make love to her more often.

Holly was literally crazy about Sebastian, she knew that.
She thought he was the most beautiful person she had ever
seen. Or touched. These days, she wept to remember the exceptional smoothness of all his body skin, the perfect small
patch of hair on his chest, so soft and fine. In the night, when
they were together, she used sometimes to reach to stroke his
back—to no avail, he almost never turned to her. Or if he did
it was with a reluctant sigh.

His presence became a tease to Holly; he was constantly
tantalizing, simply being there. And once he had gone, his
absence, especially in bed, was horrible.

So fixated was she on Sebastian ("A true addiction," she had
said more than once to Mary. "So that now I'm in withdrawal")
that she had not thought much about herself. A slight, fair
girl when they married, when Sebastian found her so pretty,
cute, Holly as a neglected wife had felt herself grow heavier.
She thought she sagged all over.

And in that neglected phase, to make her feel even uglier,
some ugly physical things began to go wrong with her. Pain,
colitis. It was all very neurotic, probably (Sebastian said she
was being neurotic. "Slavic," he called her behavior). But still
her symptoms had to be checked out. (Mary insisted that she
go to someone.) And so she went to Jonathan Green, who took
everything she said very seriously, listening with his great dark
sympathetic eyes. Jonathan, who seemed to like her and not

think that she was crazy, even having heard and seen all the worst of her. Her rejected body.

Now anticipating Jonathan as a lover (well, of course she was, of course that was what she was doing), Holly thought that if Jonathan loved her, or even just liked her a lot, it would mean she was all right. An okay person. Even, once more, possibly, cute.

"It's great, the house is getting to look a lot more like you. Less Sebastian." Mary, arrived for a drink, had been looking around.

"Well, that's what I had in mind. He always wanted everything so bare. But you know, this is really a little sick. I'm doing it all for Jonathan Green. And that's crazy, that's as bad as doing everything for Sebastian."

"Not quite. Jonathan is a much nicer person."

"We hope." Holly had begun to see herself as chasing a rainbow named Jonathan Green, and all from an idea of Mary's that could easily be wrong ("I think Jonathan Green is interested in you"). She was in a sort of frenzy, she recognized that.

Mary now said, "As a matter of fact I will have another glass of wine. What the hell, I'm getting so fat it hardly matters."

"Oh Mary, you're not." Mary, a tall, dark, strong woman looked more or less the same to Holly, always. However, looking now more closely, she saw that Mary had indeed put on a few pounds. And she thought, Oh dear, I've been so upset, so self-absorbed that I haven't really looked at Mary.

However, over their second drinks Mary seemed okay, her old self. "Actually, you and Jonathan could get married right in this house," she said. "And I'll take pictures and send them along to Sebastian, that'll really thrill him. And I'll make the cake and the wedding food, and Mark will give you away, and I'll be friend of honor."

"Mary, come on, that's not even funny."

"Yes, it is. And after the wedding we'll all live very happily ever after. Take trips together, all that nerdy middle-aged stuff. Cruises, when we get really old. How would you feel about having children with Jonathan?"

"Mary, cut it out!" But Holly was laughing too, and actually, she was also thinking, why not? She could marry again, if her lawyer ever pulled himself together and had papers served on Sebastian, as he was supposed to be doing. And she could have children. Why not with Jonathan Green? So handy, his being a doctor.

"Maybe you're right, I need a doctor around the house," she said to Mary.

"Well, I think Jonathan should be really grateful that we've got his life all worked out for him," said Mary finally.

Five more days, still, until the famous date. And Holly found that instead of talking to Sebastian in her head, or to Mary, she was having very long, silent, and extremely interesting (to her) conversations with Jonathan Green.

"So typical, his leaving me with this stupid name," Holly in her mind told Jonathan. "Holly Jones, of all the plain-Jane names. Whereas Sebastian Jones has a lot of style, don't you think? I should have kept my old name, but is Jewerelsky really any better? I don't know. Maybe it doesn't matter, after all."

And she told him, "I think I'm sort of like a convalescent

person. Getting better from something serious. I do okay and then I have a kind of relapse. Isn't that what people do when they're getting well?" She liked the medical analogy, something Jonathan would appreciate, she thought.

She did not tell Jonathan about the form of those relapses: the crying. Hours, sometimes whole days, it seemed, of tears. Unable to stop, she found it impossible too to phone for help, not even to Mary. Holly hated those tears, she hated crying. It was like some loathsome disease, incapacitating, shameful.

She wondered if she would ever be able to make love to another man without weeping for Sebastian. Sometimes she thought that she could not, and she despaired.

Preparing for Jonathan, their date, she tried not to think of tears, of crying. She concentrated on household tasks, her house.

"In summer it's really wonderful," she told Jonathan Green, in her mind. "All the flowers outside in bloom, the breezes, the cool. And it's great having so much space." But what was this, an advertisement for her house? Did she want him to come and live there?

In the two days immediately preceding the date, Holly changed her mind several dozen times on the two crucial issues of what to serve for dinner, and what to wear.

"Make something really simple, obviously," Mary counseled. "A good make-ahead stew, I could give you a new recipe I've been doing. And have lots of flowers all over. You might as well wear something pretty, maybe one of those long silk numbers?"

Good advice, but it still left considerable latitude for obsessive thought, which Holly gave it. Which stew? What kind of flowers? And which long silk dress, the blue or the black?

And Holly knew, intelligent, streetwise Holly knew all along that she was making (dangerously) too much of this. Much too much. She was asking for trouble, begging for it, she knew that she was.

She almost began to hope that Jonathan would have to break the date, or forget it.

Jonathan not only did not forget, he arrived quite promptly at seven. Hearing his car, a new Porsche, then observing his approach as he walked up the path to her house and came across the porch, Holly half-consciously made two notes: one, he looks nervous, his shoulders are tight. And, two, why is he wearing that pink sweater? She herself was wearing the long black silk, much too dressed up but too late now to change.

At her door they shook hands, both said how nice to see each other, as though it were accidental. And in a quick agitated way Jonathan took in her house.

"What a nice big place," he said, with what looked like a tiny shiver, as Holly thought, He doesn't like it. Well, neither do I, actually.

Seated, he accepted a glass of Perrier.

"A nice big house," he repeated, once they were settled with drinks.

He is wearing that sweater to make himself look younger, was what Holly was thinking. At a certain point Sebastian had begun to wear a lot of pink.

"Where are you living now?" Holly asked Jonathan.

"Well, it's a little complicated. I'm still in what was the family house. My wife, the children, school . . ." He said all this at some length, managing curiously to omit saying where he lived.

Jonathan was fairly handsome, better-looking than Holly had previously observed. However, she reminded herself, I was so hung up on the beauty of Sebastian that I didn't notice any male attractiveness, only his. I only saw Sebastian.

Jonathan's eyes were large and very dark. Very unlike Sebastian's narrow, gold-brown eyes.

"Does it feel better when a divorce is sort of finalized?" Holly attempted, thinking that divorce or separation was actually what they most had in common, at that time.

Rather defensively Jonathan told her, "Mine's nowhere near final. In fact, we're still in the very early stages. Thrashing things out. Kicking the ball around." He grinned, as though to assure her of the non-seriousness of his divorce.

His face was better in its serious phase, Holly decided. The grin was too much just that, a grin. So many large healthy white teeth that you missed his eyes, by far his best feature.

It was impossible now to imagine the long easy fluid talk that Holly had silently enjoyed with him, all those conversations in her head. Whatever had they talked about? She could no longer remember, even.

"How about dinner?" she asked. "It's not too early? It's all sort of ready, won't take a minute."

Jonathan looked at his watch and they both saw: 7:30. "Fine by me," he said.

Mercifully alone in her kitchen, Holly faced or tried to face the fact of this awkward evening. She was pleased at the degree to which she could accept its semi-failure. Not her fault, and it meant nothing, really. Just two people shy with each other, in an unaccustomed situation. Jonathan as a doctor, her doctor, was of course considerably more assured. Good at his work, always knowing what to say.

And Holly herself could be fairly animated, talkative, although it felt like rather a long time since she had been so.

Steak-and-kidney pie. A favorite of Sebastian's, and received enthusiastically by Jonathan, at first. "What a great crust!"

But Holly next noticed that he was picking out pieces of steak, avoiding the kidney. She supposed that she should have asked, but still she would not have expected that sort of squeamishness from a doctor. On the other hand, why not? Maybe doctors are more squeamish, really, than other people are? And with considerably more reason, so much exposure to visceral ugliness.

"This house can get awfully cold in the winter, though," Holly found herself babbling (obviously they would do well not to talk about the food). "Drafts everywhere. Damp."

"It feels very comfortable." Courteous Jonathan. And then, conversationally, "In your settlement, you get the house?"

"Uh?"

"The house. It's yours now?"

"Well, not exactly. I mean, I'm not sure yet. My lawyer—"

"Oh. Lawyers." Jonathan's mouth curled.

Are they really so much worse than doctors? Holly did not ask this.

.   .   .

Jonathan chose not to have dessert. "Got to stay in shape." He grinned, and then, "Help you with the dishes?"

"Oh, no. Just go on in the living room. I'll bring coffee. Decaf?"

"Please."

Holly brought in the coffee, which was unaccountably cool. They sat sipping at it as Holly thought again, Well, so much for that. How silly I was. And whenever will he go?

Instead of going, though, Jonathan Green moved closer to her, on the sofa where they sat. Very gently he put one arm around her, and then still very gently he began to kiss her. Their mouths were open, but not in an urgent way. Just kissing, hungrily (at least Holly kissed hungrily, she had not kissed anyone for so long), but the hunger seemed for more kissing. No question of anything further.

At some point Jonathan murmured near her ear, half laughing, "High school."

"Yes." And Holly thought, This is perfect, this is what I really wanted. All this tender kissing, this is what I've missed. Much more than sex. To his ear she whispered, "Jonathan, I really like you."

It went on and on, this gentle semi-greedy kissing, along with mild back-stroking caresses. Touching Jonathan's shoulders, which were broad, strong-feeling, Holly was intensely aware of maleness, such very male shoulders. Another quality she had missed.

After what could have been an hour of this occupation (impossible to tell about the time), Jonathan, still gentle, began to start to disentangle himself. He still clung to her—or was it that he allowed her to cling? No way to remember that, later on.

At last they stood kissing at the door. Good night.

"I must see you very soon" was what Jonathan said. "I'll call you."

And Holly went off happily to bed, leaving the dishes and thinking, How nice, that was just right. How nice Jonathan is, after all. I was right about him, sort of.

But the next day, on waking, Holly's first thought was that Jonathan would not call. She knew this as surely as she had always known, in her bones, that eventually Sebastian would leave her.

Her bedroom that morning was fiercely cold. Sharp winds blew through as outdoors, beyond the shuddering French windows, rain dripped from everything, from heavy rhododendron leaves, from ferns and winter weeds.

If Jonathan had stayed over, had slept there with her, there would now be another warm body in her bed. Sometimes Holly had thought that was what she most missed of Sebastian, simple bodily warmth. On the other hand, perhaps it was just as well that Jonathan had not stayed; he would not like this awakening to cold drafts, probably.

I hate this house, Holly thought as she forced herself up and out of bed. Off to do last night's dishes, to make her small breakfast.

"It was, well, sort of nice" was how Holly described the evening to Mary, who of course called to see how things had gone. "No big deal, in fact he's not the easiest guy in the world to talk to. But at the end it was, well, nice. Affectionate."

"Well, that's nice. I don't see why you're so sure you won't hear from him."

"I just am." For one thing, it's after noon, he must have

been up for hours by now, he could have called. Holly did not say this, although it was much in her mind.

"Well, in any case he's a start," said Mary ambiguously.

At least we didn't actually make love, Holly also later thought. Or would that in a way have been better? Would Jonathan be more apt to call if we had? And come to think of it, why didn't we? Does he go out with a lot of women, and only make love to one, or maybe two? Is he into safe sex, scared of AIDS?

Over the years, in waiting rooms and on planes, Holly had seen articles about men who take you to bed and then never call, no matter what they said. But she could not remember any proposed solutions. Especially not after just kissing.

Should you call him, pretending that it doesn't matter who calls whom?

"Oh, Holly. Well, I should have called you yesterday" was available Jonathan's instant response, the next morning (Holly had told his nurse that this was a "social" call, and was nevertheless put through right away).

"Well, I decided it didn't matter who called whom," Holly lied. "But I was thinking about this weekend. I sort of feel like cooking again." (Another lie, she did not feel at all like cooking. She felt like more kissing, perhaps a long slow progress into bed.)

"Well, this weekend. Not good at all. I'm on call, beeper always going off. Such a nuisance. Seeing my kids on Sunday. But next week, first thing. I'll call you."

.   .   .

Hanging up from that conversation, on Thursday morning, Holly thought, I really cannot bear this. I cannot get through until Monday. Anxiety is the worst of all, worse even than grief. And, as she sometimes used to do, in the early days of knowing Sebastian was gone, Holly took to her bed, with a pile of magazines. Getting up from time to time to heat a can of soup, or make tea.

She cried, so that even calling Mary was out of the question.

And whether she wept for Sebastian or for Jonathan seemed hardly to matter.

On Friday her lawyer called. "You sound terrible" was his comment.

"Well yes, this cold. I can't seem to shake it." Not an inventive lie, but it served.

"Well, there's a lot of flu around. Have you called your doctor?"

"No."

"You should. Anyway, I have some news that may cheer you up." His good news was that Sebastian, in New York, had signed papers: a quitclaim to the house, in return for assurances (elaborate, binding) of no further claims, ever, on him or his estate. No alimony. No-fault divorce.

"He must be planning to marry someone else." Holly had only dimly thought of this before.

"Sounds like it. Well, I guess you're in no mood for a visit. I have to be in Marin, and I thought—"

"No. Thanks."

For Holly that Saturday represented a sort of nadir, given over to pain. Bad thoughts. Self-pity. Solitude.

On Sunday, Mary called, and she too commented, "You don't sound very good."

"I don't feel too great." Holly then described her conversation with Jonathan, and finished by asking, "Why am I so sure he was lying?"

"Maybe because he was," Mary contributed (too quickly? had she seen him somewhere, with someone?). And then, possibly to change the subject, she continued, "You really sound bad. Have you considered taking your temperature?"

She told Holly about a party in Sausalito the night before, mainly colleagues of Mark's, at which, Holly thought, she could easily have seen Jonathan Green. With whoever.

On Monday, Holly conceded that actually something physical could be wrong with her; she had chills, aches in all her joints, and an entire sense of bodily weakness. She did take her temperature, which was 102 degrees.

The fact of an actual illness with a probable diagnosis, flu, was cheering. To go back to bed would be sensible, a yielding to the superior claims of illness rather than to sheer self-indulgence.

Quite early on Monday night the phone rang, and there was Jonathan Green, right on schedule—as he had said, first thing in the week.

"Odd you should call," Holly told him. "I have a sort of high fever, a hundred and two degrees. Flu, I guess."

"Well, that is pretty high. More of a child-sized fever than one we see in adults. What do you have around, medicine-wise?"

Having ascertained that she had nothing in the house beyond aspirin and cough drops, Jonathan said he would be right over.

"Okay, but Jonathan, I feel really terrible. I mean, I don't feel up to getting dressed." No long black silk, she added to herself.

"Oh, that's okay. Consider this a house call." He chuckled.

Holly changed into a prettier nightgown (cotton, nothing sexy), a good robe, and settled in the living room to wait for him.

By this time she had taken down most of Sebastian's paintings and stacked them in a closet, and had put books up on the shelves (eccentric Sebastian was fond of bare bookcases, empty shelves). There was a sheaf of magazines on the table, and flowers. Still, the room looked bare and cold, Holly thought. So large, it dwarfed every effort at warmth, and color.

She heard the car, and then the footsteps of Jonathan Green. A somewhat distant handshake at the door would be right, she thought, getting up.

Going to the door, extending her hand as she had intended, Holly found herself instead embraced. Chastely, perhaps paternally, but still, there she was, enfolded in the arms of Jonathan. For one moment.

In the living room, though, he seated himself quite apart from her, choosing the chair adjacent to the sofa where she sat (where they had spent all that time necking, before). And in a kindly, interested way, he listened to her description of her symptoms. He had even brought along some magic remedies, which he took out from a pocket: samples of antibiotics, Tylenol, cough medicine.

Holly was touched by what seemed simple human kindness. He was nice, after all.

Their medical business over, Jonathan even seemed inclined to stick around. He was looking forward to the end of winter, he told her, stretching long legs before him. Spring skiing, sailing. Baseball. His wife had not been very interested in those pursuits, and so he hoped that this year he could put in more time in that way. He grinned.

Had he guessed that Holly was not exactly a sports fan either? She rather imagined that he had, and even that she was forgiven. But she also imagined, or perceived, that he no longer saw her as a woman to kiss on a sofa. However, to some degree Holly dismissed all her crowding intuitions regarding Jonathan. After all, she was sick.

It was, though, all around a pleasant conversation, far easier than their halting, strained attempts at dinner. And then Jonathan got up to go.

At the door he embraced her again, more briefly than before. "I'll call you tomorrow," he said.

About what? Holly wondered, as she shivered in bed a short time later. And then she answered her own question, About my flu, that's what. That's what he finds interesting in me. What he likes best, now.

She was then assailed by familiar, painful thoughts of Sebastian. His beauty, and his terrible, implacable indifference to her. But she did not, as she so often had before, engage in imagined conversations with Sebastian. Perhaps she had said it all already? Nor did she cry.

Jonathan called the next day to see how she was.

"My fever's gone down. Your magic pills seem to work."

"Good. Well, I'll call you tomorrow."

.   .   .

On the night that he came to dinner, when they had sat there necking, why had he not gone on to take her to bed? This was something that Holly pondered, in her illness. Something that she could discuss with no one. Not even with Mary.

Because she was old and fat, was that it? And Jonathan knew just how old and fat she was, he had seen her, everything about her was down in his charts. That could be the explanation, but in that case why kiss her at all? He didn't have to, under the circumstances, he could have just been a very polite, onetime dinner guest.

Or was it because he did not want to commit himself to that extent? In a rational way, this made more sense. It was even a little too rational for Holly, who after all had the flu.

A day or so later, kind Mary came over with mushroom soup and some home-baked bread, and a basket of fruit, grapes and peaches and papayas. They sat in Holly's living room, in some rare February sunshine, a brief false spring. They talked.

And at last Holly asked her friend, "I really wonder whatever gave you the idea that Jonathan liked me."

"Well—" To Holly's surprise, Mary, who never blushed, now did so, a slow red flush that rose on her neck. "Well," Mary said, "that may have been a small case of wishful thinking on my part. And a little simplistic. You know, someone nice to replace mean Sebastian. And there was Jonathan, just getting a divorce, and nice. I thought."

"He is nice, in a way." He had called every day about Holly's flu, which was considerably better. Now she was just a little weak, and slightly light-headed. "I still don't quite see why Jonathan," she persisted, for no good reason. Giddily, perhaps.

"Well." Amazingly, Mary's flush deepened. "I have to admit I had the smallest crush on him myself. He is sort of, uh, cute."

"I guess." They both laughed nervously.

"And then," Mary went on, "there is this sexual fix we all seem to have on doctors. Little kids playing doctor, all that. Even before Mark, I always liked doctors, remember?"

"Yes." But Holly found herself uncomfortable in this conversation. It had gone far enough, she felt. She did not want to discuss Mary's possible crushes—nor, in a general way, sexuality.

Mary may well have felt the same, for she next asked, "What you have to do now is put on a little weight. Do you know how skinny you are? You look like that model we used to use, remember? Miss Anorexia?"

"But me? You've got to be kidding."

"I'm not, take a look at yourself."

Restored to their more usual tone, both women were happier. "I'll start by eating that whole loaf of bread you brought," Holly told Mary. "It smells fantastic."

Late one night in March, Holly's phone rang—shrill, an alarm that cut into her already unsettled sleep.

"Hello." A male voice that she did not instantly recognize, but that in a moment she knew could only be Sebastian's voice.

"Oh. Hi." Sitting up in bed, Holly pulled the covers around her shoulders. It was spring, but the nights were still very cold, and damp.

"Well, you don't sound too welcoming, but I really can't say that I blame you. Or not very much. I don't blame you very much." The slightest slur informed Holly that Sebastian was very drunk—of course he was, at three in the morning, New York time.

He laughed, and Holly heard the familiar contempt in his laugh. "I just wondered how you were," he said. "You and my house."

"I'm okay," Holly told him. "And I guess I'm going to put the house up for sale." Strangely, she had not known this was her plan until she said it to Sebastian.

He exploded, as she may have meant him to do. "Christ, do you have any idea how dumb that is? A valuable house, more valuable—Christ, how stupid can you get?"

"I need the money," she told him. "And I really don't like it here."

"You don't even know what you like! Ignorant Slavs—"

Holly replaced the receiver into its cradle, then reached down to unplug the cord. She was trembling, but only a little.

Several times later that night, in the course of her troubled sleep, she heard the dim sound of the living-room phone, which rang, and rang.

Nevertheless, in a way that she could not quite understand, the next day Holly felt considerably better. Even rested.

"I'm definitely going to move back to the city," she told Mary, over the phone. "Maybe back to our old neighborhood. I want to go back to school."

"North Beach is impossible now." Unenthusiastic Mary.

"Well, with the money from this house I could even go to Pacific Heights. Then I'd be close to the bridge. To Marin."

Mary laughed. "You're right. I just don't want you to leave. But I agree that's what you should do."

For no particular reason—she had not been thinking of

their doctor—Holly next asked, "What do you hear these days about Jonathan Green?"

"Oh, we sort of see him around. Mark and I do. You know, doctor parties."

Mary's tone had been rather studiedly vague, Holly thought, and so she pursued it. "With whom?" she asked Mary. "Surely not his wife?"

"Oh no, I think that's all over. But Jonathan seems to be into the very young. Lord, the last one looked about sixteen."

"She's probably really forty but works out all the time. Plays baseball."

They both laughed.

"What men don't know," Mary told Holly, "or one of the things they don't know is how old those kids make them look. The contrast can be cruel."

"I wonder if that's what Sebastian is up to."

"The dumb shit, I wouldn't put it past him."

That conversation took place around noon, a time of day when they often made contact, Holly and Mary.

In the course of that afternoon, Holly gave somewhat fleeting thought both to Jonathan and to Sebastian.

Of Sebastian she thought, I haven't cried for a couple of weeks. I wouldn't dare say that the pain is absolutely gone, very likely it won't ever be. It's something I have to live with, probably, the way some people have bad backs or trick knees. Ten years is just not a dismissible part of my life.

Of Jonathan she thought, How crazy that all was, pinning all those fantasies on him when he's just a plain ordinary doctor. But what did he imagine that I would be, she wondered, that I wasn't? Rich, possibly, in a house that was more to his liking? Better at talking, funnier? God knows he can't have thought I'd be younger or prettier, Jonathan already knew what I looked like.

In the later afternoon, near dinnertime, as though telepathically summoned, Jonathan called Holly. She had not heard from him since the end of her flu, a couple of weeks ago.

And that is what he asked about. "How's your flu?"

"Well, it seems to be all better. Just a little cough sometimes."

"You'd better be careful, if you're still coughing. I've seen some people down with it for a second or even a third time."

"Oh, how terrible." But why tell me about them? Holly wondered.

"And then there's a brand-new strain of flu that we're seeing. A really bad one. But if you come down with that we've got a pill that works."

"Jonathan, I don't understand what you're saying."

"I just meant, if you get this new flu we have a specific for it."

"Oh." Is that what you called about? she wanted to ask. Instead she ventured, "Well, how've you been, otherwise?" Was this a social call? Was she supposed to make small talk?

Apparently not. Very briskly Jonathan told her, "Fine, really great in fact. Well, I just wanted to be sure you're okay."

"Well, I seem to be. As far as I know, I don't have the new flu. Yet."

He seemed to grasp that a small joke had been intended, and gave her a little laugh. "So far so good," he said.

And minutes after that they said goodbye.

It was nice to hear from you, I guess, is what Holly thought.

And for some minutes she wondered just what had moti-
vated that call. Simple curiosity as to how she was? A medical
need to warn her about relapses and the dangerous new kind
of flu? Or had he wanted to find her sick, and needing him in
that way?

Any answer to any of those questions was possible, Holly
decided, and she thought that Jonathan himself did not know,
really, why he had called. In his own mind, probably, he was
just a doctor checking on a patient who had been quite sick,
with a child-sized fever.

Fleetingly, she wondered whether he would send her a bill.

He did. It arrived, perhaps by coincidence, the following day.
House call and follow-up treatment. One hundred dollars.

A NOTE ON THE TYPE

The text of this book was set in a digitized version of Garamond No. 3, a modern rendering of the type first cut by Claude Garamond (1510–1561). Garamond was a pupil of Geoffroy Tory and is believed to have based his letters on the Venetian models, although he introduced a number of important differences. It is to him that we owe the letter known as "old style." He gave to his letters a certain elegance and feeling of movement that won for their creator an immediate reputation and the patronage of Francis I of France.

Composed by Graphic Composition, Inc., Athens, Georgia

Printed and bound by R. R. Donnelley & Sons, Harrisonburg, Virginia

Typography and binding design by Dorothy Schmiderer Baker